Schultz

THE
CHINESE
GAME

THE CHINESE GAME

By Charles Larson

J. B. LIPPINCOTT COMPANY
Philadelphia and New York

To Alice

THE
CHINESE
GAME

CHAPTER 1

SUDDENLY THE weeping stopped.

On Belgard's right, Corporal Fox had halted and was half turned away from the jungle, looking back down the terraced hillside toward the camp. Fox, a Negro, had covered the last ten yards at a trot; pale red dust clung to his wet face and arms like a sunburn. He moved his tongue absently over his lower lip and glanced at Belgard.

"We're going back right now," Belgard murmured. "Don't worry about it."

"No, sir."

"Do you hear anything?"

"No, Captain."

Well, we've come too far, Belgard thought, and for the first time he began to consider seriously the notion of an ambush. He never had intended to climb beyond the first terrace. But the faint sobs had seemed to be always just out of reach, only a few yards farther along in the windless haze, and there'd been such shock in them, such anguish, that he'd almost been able to see the child in the tiger's mouth.

He motioned for Fox to move out, and presently he

started his own quiet retreat, stepping backward from the edge of the paddy, eyes fixed on the raw new undergrowth along the cleared perimeter. He couldn't have said what made him pause—some blind man's response to an unexpected curb—but he did, and there in the dust at his feet lay a green velvet-covered cylinder about the size of a king-size beer can, so classic an illustration of what a booby trap ought to look like that he could do little more than blink down at it and wonder why it hadn't exploded.

Fox had dropped over the topmost level onto the broad middle terrace by now and vanished. Belgard tried to ease the side of his boot away from the cylinder, but the movement sent it bouncing in a heavy arc down the slope into a cluster of stones. After a time, he opened his stiffened lids a bare crack. The impact had jarred open the top of the cylinder; there were no wires visible at the uncovered end—no fuses, nothing but the splintered tips of a dozen or more wooden sticks.

He pondered his luck, and then he leaned in for a closer examination, but as he did, Fox let out an indistinct yell and he looked up again in annoyance. Fox continued to shout until Belgard finally glanced over his shoulder. Behind him, at the base of one of the pines, a ten-year-old naked Montagnard boy was poised with a grenade in his left hand. The pin had been pulled, but Fox's hoarse shouts had rattled the child. While the seconds ticked away, the boy stood gazing at Belgard, gray with panic, momentarily paralyzed.

"Friend," Belgard said in Rhadé, and the boy lobbed the grenade like a specter in a dream, too late for maximum effectiveness. Belgard managed to spin to his right before the detonation, and most of the shards that reached him ripped into his left thigh. The boy, by accident or instinct, had dropped to his belly behind a fallen log, but one or two chunks of metal evidently plowed through the rotten trunk because he scrambled away almost at once, his flayed, bloody back arched in stupefaction and horror.

Belgard was still screaming for him to wait when Fox galloped up, although by then the skinned child had disappeared. "Jesus, Jesus, Jesus," Fox kept grunting.

"Leave me alone!" Belgard panted. "Call Dodd—"

Fox ran.

CHAPTER 2

THE FIRST THING Sergeant Grainger said when he heard the captain had been booby-trapped was, "Fine, now maybe we can get on with the goddam war." He was a squat complicated West Virginian, rather superstitious, and he had dreamed for three nights in a row that his dead daughter, Joanne, had come into the Special Forces camp to talk to him but had backed away each time he had asked her what she wanted. The strain of waiting for something destructive to happen had affected his bowels as well as his temper, and he was in the latrine when Fox located him.

Although Fox was in considerable pain from a stitch in his side, he insisted on hobbling along while Grainger rounded up a rescue patrol. He seemed to blame himself for Belgard's accident; he said he had beseeched the captain not to touch the cylinder, but that it had been like talking to a brick wall.

"What cylinder?"

"I said, 'Why, for Christ's sake, sir, you know better than that—' "

In the 110-degree shade of the mess shack, Grainger

found a machine gunner named Elkins asleep on his air mattress. He woke him, told him what had happened, and Elkins said he'd get his weapon and meet the patrol at the north gate in five minutes.

"Where's Dodd?" Grainger bellowed after him. "Village?"

"Village," Elkins shouted back.

The unaccustomed midafternoon agitation had roused several male Montagnards; Grainger could see them peeping through the thorn barrier the captain had erected to separate the training grounds from the hamlet proper. This frail wall, unsuitable as a cobweb for its purpose, had been raised to protect the Montagnard women from American lusts. Grainger had pointed out that any lust too weak to force a thorn fence wasn't much to worry about in the first place, but the captain had replied that he required the wall anyway, that it was exactly what he wanted. He and the chieftain had spent the better part of a day dedicating it, the chief blessing the Montagnard portion with rice wine and blood and Captain Belgard clicking out his bridge periodically to tap the teeth on this or that thorn on the American side. After the fence had been declared sound and the women safe, the chief had welcomed Belgard's men to the foothills in Rhadé and Belgard had responded in the same dialect. He had promised an end to local Cong terrorism and had expressed the hope that the war would be over before the summer monsoon began. Meanwhile, he said, he brought greetings from the mandarin Diem in Saigon and the lord Kennedy in Washington, both of whom were confident that 1963 would be a year of progress and victory. He introduced Lieutenant Dodd as a medicine man who fully understood the spirits of the rocks and mountains, having been born in the mountain province of Colorado, America, and called upon Dodd to issue his magic regardless of sex or age—one vitamin capsule to each man, woman, and child each day, commencing now. Dodd stared at him in astonishment and then gazed off toward Cambodia without replying. The Montagnards shivered at this clash of wills and watched Belgard out of the corners of their Indonesian eyes. Three times Belgard thundered out his order, until Dodd, broken like a reed, gave in. The naked tribesmen could scarcely repress their sniggers as Dodd passed sullenly down the line they formed, popping a capsule into each triumphant mouth.

"Son of a bitch is a real operator, ain't he?" Fox had whispered to Grainger. "That was kind of cute how he done that."

"Gets any cuter," said Grainger, "and I may fwow up."

"Listen, man, we're up here to help the people, don't matter how."

"I'll tell you why I'm up here," Grainger said. "I'm up here because the general told me to get my *ass* up here, that's why I'm up here. I obscenity on the people."

"You what?" Fox asked.

"Forget it," Grainger said wearily.

Grainger pretended antipathy toward Belgard, because Grainger didn't understand this war, and in his heart of hearts he doubted that anyone did. He felt that American business interests were involved and that controlled police actions probably were designed to prime the Russian as well as the American economic pump, but all of this seemed too self-evident to grow apoplectic over. He was a good soldier, a craftsman, the holder of ribbons for campaigns from Luzon to Korea, and he never had understood the political purpose of any one of them. It was none of his business. It was none of Belgard's business either. Grainger distrusted passion in officers below the rank of colonel, especially when they were younger than he was.

Nonetheless, he grudgingly admired Belgard, even respected him.

He said now through the thorn fence, "Go find the Long Nose medicine man. Tell him to come to the north gate."

The somber faces grew more truculent. "Why?"

"Tell him."

"Tiger? Cong?"

"Tell him!"

The youngest man slipped away. The others stayed to study Grainger, rapt and troubled. Right, Grainger thought through a wave of fatigue: ten weeks' intensive weapons training, a .45 pistol issued to every male over the age of fifteen, enough Vietminh in the hills to mount a serious attack at any goddam given minute, and there you bare-assed bastards stand with your spears. "O.K., screw all of you," he said in English.

Fox, close on his heels as he crossed the compound, wheezed, "You talked too fast. What did you tell 'em? Something about gate—"

"They'll bring Dodd. Wait for him at the gate, fill him in. Where did the captain get it?"

"In the rice field," Fox said.

"Fox," Grainger said, "you wouldn't believe how bloody sick I am of comedians."

"Oh—legs," Fox said. "In the legs."

Elkins and a man named Rosen, whom Grainger had sent after extra grenades, were emerging from the munitions shack.

"Come on, come on, come on!" Grainger shouted, and both men broke into a sprint.

"I started to lift him up," Fox said, "carry him in, but

he told me to quit haulin' at him and go get help. What else could I do?"

"Nothing," Grainger said. "You were a great big suckling hero. You obeyed orders."

"Listen—" Fox began hotly.

The men standing alongside the guard at the outer bamboo fence fell silent when Grainger and Fox strode across the water-filled spiked moat. "How does she look?" Grainger asked.

"Very, very quiet," replied the guard. He was the camp's celebrity, a gigantic ex-dancer who had once appeared on the Ed Sullivan show. He said Ed was the sweetest guy in the world and he had promised to introduce the whole gang to him at the earliest opportunity.

The rice field rose in primitive terraces to a tangled forest a thousand yards northward.

"Where is he?" Grainger asked.

Fox pointed. "See them first pines? Right there."

Jellied shapes danced and swam across Grainger's vision. A pearl-colored haze lay over the hot slope. Squinting wouldn't penetrate it. Nothing could penetrate it. Victor Charlie, cheek pressed to his Chinese rifle, would be snug as a bug in a rug in that haze. Grainger was reminded of the Westerns he'd seen on summer Saturday afternoons, of Geronimo, patient and still, waiting for the cavalry to ride out of the fort.

"Fox," Grainger murmured, "will you kindly tell me what the two of you were doing over there in the first place?"

"Well," Fox said, "he thought he heard this little child crying."

Grainger looked around at him. Presently he said, "You're kidding me."

"I swear to God," Fox said.

Grainger glanced at the guard, and the guard said, "All right, what was I supposed to do? He's the captain. I can't hit him over the head. I opened the gate."

"Elkins," Grainger said at last.

"Yoh."

"Straight up the middle, stretcher-bearers behind you. I'll take your left flank, Rosen the right."

"Now, if we're ambushed—" Rosen began.

"We won't be ambushed," Grainger said.

"Then what's all this security crap for?"

"Drill," Grainger said, "to keep you aggravated." He motioned, and set out on a line to Elkins's left, hearing the trumpets blare from the far-off screen in the hushed and darkened movie house.

CHAPTER 3

THE MUFFLED CLANK of gear brought Belgard's head around, but he was unable to spot the approaching patrol from his position under the trees. At the explosion, he'd been looking west toward the child, and that was the direction in which he'd collapsed, head on the up side of the incline, legs crumpled beneath him. After Fox had left, he'd tried to twist onto his back, but his abdominal muscles had failed to respond and he'd been forced to remain face down in the dirt, wondering whether the slickness along his groin was urine or sweat or blood.

In the field below, the minimal patrol sounds stopped. Grainger had paused to sniff the wind. Belgard knew now for a fact that it had to be Grainger in command. Dodd would have realized that there was a time for caution and a time for impulse. Dodd never would have allowed a man to bleed to death while he secured an empty rice paddy.

Belgard rubbed the dust away from his nose and eyes and surveyed the dense undergrowth beyond the pines. If the boy had not been too badly mangled—if he had not fallen dead somewhere just out of sight—he could of course have made contact by now with the men who had sent him. An experienced guerrilla commander would take swift advantage of the bait Belgard represented, and the officers who had led the crack Sixtieth and Eightieth North Vietnamese battalions down the Ho Chi Minh trail in 1961 and 1962 were highly experienced.

Mosquitoes sang through the oppressive haze, but there was no other sound, no other movement. Soon the muted jingle of metal on metal recommenced. A gleam of pain cut like a sword stroke across the fleshy part of Belgard's left calf; he dropped his forehead onto the red earth again. Fool, he thought, posturing fatheaded fool—fifteen men endangered, hundreds of villagers, because you know more than the manual. A crying child, for the love of God. A ploy that must have been ancient when the kids of Gaul had used it on the Roman Legions. Fantastic. It was going to make a captivating report for Major Finney to read in Ton That. "One: At approximately fifteen hundred hours this date, Captain Belgard, together with Corporal Fox, left the compound in order to seek out and comfort a crying Moi child. Two: The reason for this unorthodox action—"

Belgard blew his breath out. It didn't matter. Finney wouldn't understand in any event. But then few people would. Cookie, he thought, would. It had been a tough six months for Cookie. She had liked Augsberg. She'd been clearly worried when Belgard told her about his decision to transfer to Vietnam, but she said she'd known what she was getting into when she'd married a West Pointer, and if Belgard wanted to go that route, then that's what she wanted too. She'd left to stay with her folks in Glendale, and she sent Belgard a letter every week and a little gift every month. Belgard touched the soft scented hair in fancy and kissed the beautiful eyes....

Stabbing, sizzling, the pain caught this time at his knee. He gripped the ground until his knuckles were white, and finally the torment eased, though not altogether. He was reminded of the dark line made by waves on the sand when the tide was coming in—never greatly higher, but always a little higher.

Even so, it was difficult for him to believe that he'd been badly wounded. The numbness in his lower belly, for instance, he attributed to shock. His first concern, on seeing the grenade sail toward him, had been for his genitals, and he suspected that they were his main concern still, psychologically, but that if they had been seriously damaged he would have been unconscious instead of numb.

In the forest above him and to his left, Grainger murmured, "Rosen?" and Rosen, on the right, answered, "Check, she's clear."

"Rosen?" Belgard grunted.

"Yes, sir."

He spat dust out of his mouth and raised his head painfully. "There's a log a little further on this way—see it?"

"Yes, sir."

"Look around there for a dead child—boy about ten."

Grainger eased out of the green undergrowth. He waved for Elkins and the stretcher-bearers to come forward, and then he squatted beside Belgard. "All right, put your head down," he muttered. "Stay quiet. How do you feel?"

"Where's Dodd?"

"On his way."

Both of them, Belgard thought, sounded sullen and constrained, as embarrassed by this contretemps as if he'd spilled a drink on a new rug at a party.

Grainger had begun to slit his left pants leg with a knife. "Can you move your toes?"

"Yeah—"

"Feel this?"

"Yes."

"This?"

"Yes!"

"Well," Grainger said, "you didn't bust anything." He straightened. "Lay the stretcher along his side," he said to the men standing at his feet. "When I say 'three' roll him over."

"I can't seem to feel much around my lower stomach, though," Belgard said. "Is there any blood down there?"

After a moment, Grainger said, "What do you mean, much? Can you feel anything at all?"

"Not a lot. Is that serious?"

"No, no," Grainger said. He squatted down again. "You want to turn over now?"

Belgard tried until his ears rang, but it was no use. "I can't quite make it. Give me a hand—"

"Open your mouth," Grainger said. He smoothed out a bent cigarette, put it between Belgard's lips, and lit it.

Belgard took one or two puffs in silence and then grimaced, and Grainger removed the cigarette. A stream of dirt rattled down the hillside; he craned his neck. It was Rosen returning. "What'd you find?" Belgard asked.

"Looks like a butcher shop up there," Rosen said.

"See the boy?"

"All I saw was blood, Captain."

"That means he got away," Belgard said. "Let's clear out. Grainger?"

"Was the kid alone, Captain?" Grainger asked.

"Alone, yes—"

"What did he do, hand you the cylinder? Throw it?"

"What cylinder?"

"I don't know, Fox said something—"

"No, no," Belgard said, "he had a grenade. I was looking at this other damn thing. But it was all right, it wasn't wired. It was a box full of sticks. Fox yelled—"

Grainger frowned. "Sticks?"

"Bamboo, flat—"

"Like tongue depressors? About that size?"

"Well, longer—"

"Did they have Chinese characters printed at one end?" Grainger's voice had become intent and pressing.

Irritated, Belgard said, "Oh, Christ, Grainger, I don't remember."

"Where is this box?"

"Down there somewhere." Belgard braced his hands on the ground close to him, chest high. "Rosen, help me roll over—"

"Wait a minute, here they come," Grainger said. He moved a little way down the slope, motioning toward the camp.

"Rosen," Belgard repeated.

"Yes, sir."

"Keep him quiet, Nate," Grainger said.

Astounded, Belgard said, "What are you bucking for, Sergeant—a court-martial?"

"No, sir."

"Then quit futzing around! I've got one, two, five men —I've got a third of my force—exposed like ducks on a pond, I've got a hamlet full of Montagnards to defend if some bright-eyed bastard decided to press his advantage and attack—"

Someone ran in on his blind side, and he swiveled his head as Lieutenant Dodd knelt down, snapping open his medical kit. "Well, well, well," Dodd said in a hearty low tone. "Captain fall down and go boom?" Perspiration had soaked his thin blouse and darkened the waist of his trousers; his face was moist and ashen. Dodd was a little too stout to go racing up hills under an Asiatic sun. He was twenty-two—six years younger than Belgard—and his avocational interests lay largely in the arts rather than in Belgard's fields of politics and science, but they'd discovered that they had both attended the same grammar school in Santa Rosa, and a warm friendship had flowered in the rich soil of their mutual hatred for a mathematics teacher named Tibbets. Dodd had studied premed at the University of Oregon in order to prepare himself to enter the family undertaking business, and he had a fair grasp of basic pathology. In the first month of the camp's existence he had exhausted thirteen medical kits, but he had cleared up all the trachoma in the village, all of the pneumonia, and most of the malaria. He had been bemused at first by the sight of the Moi kids running around holding their heads; he had thought it was a Montagnard custom. But when the small boys had grown to trust him, he learned that they were holding their heads in pain—that each suffered from ears that continually ran with pus. It had taken him three weeks to abolish the infection most of them had endured all their lives. His only failure so far had been in obstetrics. The native women would accept pills from him, but neither threats nor cajolery nor guile had yet persuaded them that he should be allowed to attend their confinements. Only five days before, the village's luck finally had run out. The midwives had dropped a baby in scalding water and killed it and, in their dismay, had run wailing out of the hut and left the new fourteen-year-old mother to bleed to death. The two unexpected fatalities had cast a pall of superstitious gloom over the entire tribe; one more in the same week would force the people to abandon this village, to establish another miles away and never again return to the blighted area.

It was a contingency that haunted both Dodd and Belgard, and it was the unorthodox reason why Belgard had gone seeking a lost Moi child in tiger country.

Humming, Dodd probed at Belgard's torn leg. "This is a real mess, isn't it?" he said. "Looks like you stuck it in a Waring mixer. Hurt any?"

"It smarts some, yeah," Belgard ground out.

"Well," Dodd said, "I think she ought to sew up pretty good. Provided I can find my thread. I don't suppose you'd let me amputate. That's what I need the practice in."

"Why not? I mean, I've *got* two of 'em—"

"*Right*," Dodd said. "Take a breath."

Belgard did, and barely felt the hypodermic needle enter.

Dodd put a hand on his shoulder. "Okay, you'll be fine. Few days off down in Pleiku—"

"No need to evacuate back to Saigon?"

"Oh, I wouldn't think so," Dodd said.

"Do you send in separate reports to Ton That, Leonard, or how does that work?"

"I'm supposed to," Dodd replied. "Why?"

Belgard was silent for a few seconds, weighing his words. Then he said, "Finney's getting a little short over here. Did you know that?"

"Is that right?"

"His tour ends in July. He told me he didn't think he'd extend."

"Oh," Dodd said.

Belgard glanced up at him. "The fact is, I really don't

want to rock the boat any more than I have to right now."

"Naturally not."

"Do you follow me?"

"No, I don't," Dodd said.

"Well," Belgard said, "Finney wasn't too happy about starting this camp in the first place. I think we're doing a lot of good work."

"So do I."

"But you might say I went out on a limb. I picked the spot. I pushed the request through channels. I didn't exactly go over Finney's head—"

"Now I follow you," Dodd said.

"I don't say he'd ask Saigon to abandon the whole project," Belgard went on, "if he found out I was flat on my back, but it might make him a little uneasy."

"Like a pansy chicken with its head cut off," Dodd said.

"Finney's all right," Belgard began. "He's just got a lot on his mind."

"Bull shit," Dodd said. "The only thing Finney's got on his mind is a full crop of curly black hair. Ignorant butt-scratching sadist." He sat back on his heels and banged his kit closed.

"Rosen," Belgard said.

"Yes, sir."

"Don't hover, you make me nervous. Did Grainger post any lookouts?"

"Yes, sir."

"Where is he?"

"Edge of the paddy, Captain. I think he's trying to find the cylinder you told me about."

"Go help him."

Dodd's eyes followed Rosen broodingly until he was out of earshot and then returned to Belgard's face.

"Mister," Belgard said, "I don't ever want to hear a statement like that out of you again, you understand me? If you can't control your tongue, you keep your mouth shut."

Dodd flicked dust off the bottom button of his shirt and then wound his watch, cheeks crimson.

"All right," Belgard continued, "when you write your report, try to make it as reasoned and unemotional as possible. State exactly what happened but don't over-emphasize the severity of the wound and don't—you know—dwell on any temporary incapacity that—"

"Wait a minute, isn't this Wednesday?" Dodd asked.

"Wednesday?"

"Let's see, the chopper won't be in until day after tomorrow. . . . I don't think I'll get to the report anyhow until Monday or Tuesday—I want to keep an eye on Fox's tonsils. If we miss the week-end mail pickup—"

"Well, try not to miss it," Belgard said, "but don't kill yourself if you do. You know your own best pace."

"Yes, sir."

Belgard let his cheek drop onto the back of his hand. His lower stomach had begun to throb faintly at last, and the widening ache was as reassuring to him as it was uncomfortable. He debated over whether or not to bring the matter to Dodd's attention and then decided not to since the numbness was certainly leaving, and Dodd had enough on his mind as it was.

"Captain," Grainger said almost in his ear. "Captain? Captain!"

Electrified, Belgard jerked his head up.

"Do you know what this thing *is?*" Grainger asked. He had recovered the cylinder. He held it at arm's length, his pale blue eyes wonder-struck.

Belgard, still scouring the hill for the enemy, kept

repeating, "What? What?" and trying to think what to do next, how either to make himself part of an orderly retreat or an efficient unit in the counterattack. He couldn't understand why he hadn't heard the alarm from the lookouts.

"Why, the last time I saw one of these," Grainger said, "I couldn't have been more than fifteen–sixteen years old! When was the San Francisco Fair?"

"Year my brother was born," Dodd replied. "Thirty-nine."

"Well, that's when it was then," Grainger said.

Belgard rested his chin on his hand again. A stubby black insect clambered over the ridges his gripping fingers had dug out of the red soil. "You're positive about that, are you, Howard?"

"It might have been forty," Grainger said. "Thirty-nine or forty. I believe it was thirty-nine, though."

"I see," Belgard said.

"What's the matter, did I startle you?" Grainger asked.

"Oh, a little," Belgard said.

"I'm sorry, Captain."

"That's all right," Belgard said. "But if you do it again, do you know what'll happen to you? I'll bust you, Howard. Let me put it this way. If there was a rank below private, you wouldn't even get up to *that* until the day after you retired. O.K.?"

"Yes, sir," Grainger said.

"All right, men," Dodd said briskly, "let's take him home. Be careful of the leg—"

"No belly problems, Lieutenant?" Grainger asked.

Belgard heard Dodd start to say "No what?" and then the PFC at his head hoisted his shoulders off the ground in order to roll him onto the stretcher, and the clot that had formed above his hip broke and something basic in his gut shifted, and the concurrent agony was steeper than anything Belgard ever had experienced before, a medieval torture so extraordinary that all he could do was gape at the rotating horizon, mute as a giraffe.

He fell into a partial faint; Dodd's disembodied face floated over him. "Quiet, quiet," Dodd seemed to whisper. "Is that better?"

"No—"

"Hang on a minute."

"Can you give me something—morphine—"

"I did. Hang on."

He was on his back. His cockscomb-red eyelids were too thin for the brassy sun. He tried to bring his forearm up to cover them, but he'd been strapped onto the stretcher.

"Lie still, Jack," Dodd whispered.

He had a glimpse of Grainger looming over him, shading him. "I don't believe I can stand this," he said.

"It won't be much longer now," Grainger said.

"Tell us about the cylinder, Sergeant," said Dodd. "I've never seen anything like that. What is it?"

"Well, it's a game," Grainger said. "It must have belonged to the boy. Chinese—"

"Hold it down where the captain can see."

The green velvet was worn and stained. "Look." Grainger rattled the box. Under the persistent oscillation, several of the bamboo wands rose from the pack. One teetered, toppled out.

Belgard said, "We can't stay here. We've been out here too long. What time is it?"

"Watch the sergeant," Dodd said.

"Now, step number one is to shake out your stick," Grainger said. "Right? O.K. Look at the end. All of these characters are different, different one on each wand."

"What do they mean?" Dodd asked.

"They're nouns. Like 'garden,' 'wealth,' 'island'—"

"Ah," Dodd said.

"I don't know, but say this one is 'garden.' "

"Yeah."

"So, that's the sign. Garden. I close my eyes. I imagine a door—"

"A what?" Dodd asked.

"Door—any kind of a door—and in the center of this door I draw the character for 'garden.' Time passes. The door opens. I walk through—"

"Into a garden?"

"Willow trees, fountains—"

"You've hypnotized yourself."

Elkins had come up. "Where's the Chinese character for Kim Novak?" he asked. "Hubba *hubba*."

"Crazy," Belgard mumbled. The warm earth billowed in the wind.

Dodd's finger lifted an eyelid. "How do you feel, Jack?"

"Let's dance," Belgard said. "You lead."

The friendly laughter had substance and color. It was yolk-yellow and rounded. "Try to keep him level when you raise him," Dodd said.

"Listen, you want to hear the Cong marching song?" Belgard inquired. "Hey, Grainger?"

"Yeah, Captain, what's the Cong marching song?"

" 'Hi ho,' " Belgard sang, " 'hi ho, it's off to work we go—' "

He continued to sing it all the way back to the camp. Then, as they were crossing the moat, he suddenly recalled why he'd gone to the bazaar in the first place. "Where's my game?" he said, "who's got my goddam game? Don't anybody leave the room—"

"Here it is, Captain," Grainger said. "I'm holding it for you."

"Well, see that you do," Belgard said. "My mother gave me that game." He began to weep. " 'I'd walk a million miles,' " he sang, " 'for one of your smiles, my ma-aa-aam-my.' "

CHAPTER 4

HE SLEPT until midnight. He coughed, and Dodd, who had been stealing a cat nap on the cot beside him, sat up. "Water?" Dodd asked.

"Uh?"

"Try not to cough. How's the belly?"

Belgard contemplated the slanted roof, the constricted walls. "I don't know where I am."

"This is my tent," Dodd told him. "You know me, don't you?"

"Oh, come on, Leonard, Jesus," Belgard said. He felt peevish and fretful, childlike. His stomach was sore, though the bruised pain that had characterized it before was gone. Sounds commenced to separate themselves into identities. The 81-mm mortar under the flagpole was on its nightly fire mission to keep Charlie loose. A trick of acoustics carried Grainger's commands all the way across the parade ground. "Prepare to fire." A rest. "Hang it," to order the insertion of the projectile into the tube. "Fire!" Fox was one of the crew on duty. Every gunner had a different yell. Fox's was as shrill as a girl's. He'd drop the bomb, duck into his shoelace-tying position,

close his eyes, and holler for his eardrums' sake. Merci-
fully, the detonation would drown out his shriek. The
thud fifteen hundred yards up the slope would arrive
some twenty seconds later, and the routine would start
again. "Prepare to fire—hang it—fire!"

"—by eight-thirty or nine," Dodd said, "and they'll try
to have a C-forty-seven for you in Ton That."

"What?"

"C-forty-seven," Dodd repeated. "You ought to be in
Saigon before noon with any luck at all."

"Who'll be in Saigon?" Belgard said. "I'm not going to
Saigon."

"Jack—" Dodd started.

"I'm not going to Saigon!" Belgard said.

"I can't treat a wound like that!" Dodd snapped.
"Grow up! Who do you think I am? I'm not a doctor!"
He broke off and cleared his throat. "I don't know what
caused the local paralysis. It may have been psychologi-
cal, or the splinter may have lodged in the abdominal
muscle. All I'm sure of is that it went in and it didn't
come out. Anyway, I radioed Ton That and they'll send
over a chopper in the morning."

Belgard sighed explosively. "What did Finney say?"

"Finney wasn't there. He'd gone over to Pleiku for
some ceremony. I talked to the province chief. The
colonel. I don't know his name."

"Tai."

"What is it?"

"The Buddhist? Nguyen Van Tai."

"Yes, Tai. He said he'd fill Finney in."

The fire mission had ended. A six-foot gong vibrated in
the village, fluid, shimmering, tragic. Beneath the long
reverberations, Belgard could hear the trickle of bamboo
sticks, the muffled measured stroke of hide-covered mal-

lets on tom-toms. It was the first night since his arrival that he had not slept in the village, in the chieftain's hut.

"What did you tell the Moi? Did they see me carried in?"

"They thought you were dead. I let the chief listen to your heart. He accepted the idea that you were under a temporary spell."

"Leonard," Belgard began.

"It's going to be all right," Dodd said. "Do you want another shot?"

"No."

"What do you assume the worst for? Finney's a politician. Finney's in favor of what works. This camp works. Finney hasn't got the authority to scuttle a project that Saigon supports, anyway. You're scaring yourself with ghost stories. Aren't you also a little guilty of the sin of pride? I don't consider this Camp Belgard."

"Well, I don't either," Belgard said. But embarrassment warmed his scalp.

Dodd shifted on his cot. "I didn't mean that quite the way it sounded."

"Is that," Belgard said, "the impression I give?"

"Splendid," Dodd muttered. "Now I've wounded you."

"I'm not wounded," Belgard said.

"Listen, Jack. Everybody owns a piece of the war—that's self-evident—whether it's a hill in Eye Corps or a desk in General Harkins's file room. If they weren't convinced that their piece of ground was the center of the action, the hub of the wheel, they couldn't stand it—they'd desert or they'd die. O.K. They believe and they dig in. But they aren't gods. They didn't create the ground. They're chess pieces. So occasionally they're moved. Sometimes they're overrun. Sometimes they're sacrificed."

"Get to your point," Belgard said.

"Well," Dodd said, "I just think a chessman's a damn fool to fall in love with his square."

Belgard searched Dodd's plump face.

"What's the matter?" Dodd asked.

"Leonard, what do you know," said Belgard, "that I don't know?"

Dodd puffed his cheeks out and pressed his fingers against his tired eyes.

"You might as well tell me. I'll find out anyway," Belgard said.

"Go to sleep, Jack."

"If you think you'll be sending me to the hospital with a better mental attitude, you're wrong."

"Uh huh," Dodd said.

"Is it Finney?"

"What in the hell kind of a thing have you *got* for Finney? Finney couldn't have been nicer! He wanted to know if there was anything he could *do*, he—"

"You mean Tai," Belgard said. "Finney was in Pleiku."

"What?"

"I said Finney was in Pleiku. You meant Tai couldn't have been nicer."

"Tai," Dodd said. "Right."

"Right," Belgard repeated. "What's going on?"

The Moi gong throbbed; a second firing mission began. "Prepare to fire," Grainger said. "Hang it. Fire."

"He's flying to Saigon himself," Dodd said.

"Finney."

"Yes."

"Did he tell you why?"

"To talk to the general. He's convinced we're making a tactical mistake here."

"In what way?"

—34—

"He didn't take me into his confidence. Something about intelligence reports. I got the impression that he thought we were overextended. He seemed to feel that we'd be in trouble if the Cong were reinforced."

"If?"

"That was just an impression on my part."

"Then wouldn't it be a better idea to reinforce the camp? The Twenty-fifth Vietnamese could send a few troops from Quang Ngai. They've been blooded. They kicked hell out of the Sixtieth."

"Captain, you don't have to convince me—"

Belgard put his head back on the damp flat pillow. "Did you suggest it?"

"Yes," Dodd said.

"What did he say?"

"He reminded me that we were already into May and that the rains would be starting at any moment. He said the Twenty-fifth had eleven strategic hamlets to protect at Quang Ngai, and he asked me what I thought the effect would be on morale for the farmers to see elements of the Twenty-fifth marching off into the hills just when every able-bodied male in the complex had to be outside the barbed wire preparing and planting the seedbeds. I told him I appreciated his point, but that I thought a token force would be sufficient up here. An officer and ten or twelve men. I said I didn't believe the departure of twelve soldiers would panic the entire province, but he said he was afraid he had to disagree. The whole conversation was on a very high level, very polite."

"He wants to pull the whole team out, then."

"Yes."

"You discussed the safety of the Montagnards?"

"He wondered if they could be relocated, assimilated into Quang Ngai city. I asked him to remember that

they'd already been relocated once—that they were no-
mads—that it had been hard enough to get them to come
this far out of the mountains."

Belgard nodded.

"Now there are two points here," Dodd went on, "that
I don't think we ought to forget. First, these are just
Finney's views. Colonel Tai may not agree. After all,
Finney doesn't make policy; he's an adviser. Second, the
Montagnards themselves won't be exactly unarmed, Jack.
What have we been teaching them for the last ten weeks
if it wasn't to defend the village? They'll have the
mortars, they'll have the side arms—"

"What time is it?" Belgard asked.

"It's twenty past twelve."

"Would you tell the chief I'd like to talk to him?"

"Your mind would be clearer in the morning."

"Get him," Belgard said.

Dodd patted his feet around the wooden floor until he'd
located his shoes. Then he put them on and left the tent
silently.

The night air had grown cooler on Belgard's bare chest;
within days the pulpy clouds that had been boiling up
from the south would clear Cambodia and the rains would
start. They were late, but they were on the way. He and
Dodd and the Moi medicine man had been up to their
backsides in sorcery; if there was a spirit left unplacated,
it wasn't their fault. Over the past few days, Belgard's
bridge had been out of his mouth as often as it had been
in.

He raised his hand to cover his eyes; his elbow cracked
against the under part of a small table Dodd had placed
next to the cot, and something thumped loudly onto the
floor. Whistling, stretching his eyebrows, Belgard
clutched the elbow. In the semidarkness, he could see that

the fallen object was the Chinese game. The lid had popped off and one of the sticks had bounced out.

Belgard's first impulse was to leave the damned thing there until it rotted. He had resented Grainger's simple-minded fascination with it as well as Dodd's patronizing efforts to use it as a distraction, and he was annoyed to see it still in the tent.

He turned his face to the wall.

"Step number one," Grainger whispered in his ear, "is to shake out your stick."

The words were so vivid that Belgard was positive Grainger would be there when he turned back. "Howard?" he said.

The tent was empty. But the game had been returned to the table.

Belgard lay unmoving for a very long time.

On the opposite side of the parade ground, Grainger shouted, "Prepare to fire—hang it—fire!"

The stick itself was resting against the side of the cylinder at the edge of the table top. The ideograph on the splintered widest end of the wand seemed unbalanced and ugly. It suggested a flag, wind-whipped toward the east, flying over two spurred scissor slashes that might have represented the legs of a marching man.

Belgard rolled his head back onto the pillow and studied the shadow designs on the low tent roof and thought about Cookie until he heard Dodd returning.

The Montagnard chief entered first. He sat on his heels by the tent flap and watched Dodd cross past him to the table. "Everything copacetic?" Dodd asked.

"Len," Belgard said, "how long have you been gone?"

Dodd glanced at his watch. "About—four and a half minutes. Why?"

"Did you see anybody go in or out of the tent?"

"*This* tent?"

"Grainger?"

"Why, no, Grainger's on the mortar. Can't you hear him?"

After a moment, Belgard said, "Who's been playing with the game?"

Dodd sat down on the other cot.

"Now don't start some foolishness about who am I and all that crap!" Belgard said. "Has anybody been playing with this game?"

"Not that I know of," Dodd replied, "no."

"All right," Belgard said.

"What did you do, have a nightmare?" Dodd asked.

"No, I didn't have a nightmare," Belgard said. "I thought I knocked the game off the table, but I was wrong, apparently. It's not important."

"Well," Dodd said, "if—"

"Thanks for bringing the chief over," Belgard said. "If I want anything, I'll holler."

"Check," Dodd said.

Belgard pushed the game back so that he could see the chief's face. The velvet was cold, damp, as muscular as a snake's trunk. "The spell was short but very deep," he said to the chief in Rhadé. "I appreciate your concern."

"I hope it was dreamless."

"It was dreamless."

The chieftain, a grizzled, handsome fifty, kept his eyes on Belgard's face. He would not ask about Belgard's injuries until Belgard raised the subject himself. He was by nature a man of reticence and tact, although these qualities had brought him sorrow in the past. In 1961, he'd lost his right hand to a Cong ax because of a polite blunder. He hadn't been aware that the French problem had ended in a North-South Vietnamese quarrel, and he had delicately tried to overlook the passion of the young Viet-minh officer who had appeared in the mountains one day to recruit the Moi as guerrillas. He had told the officer that upon reflection his people had decided to remain aloof from the fight. The officer had grown tense and replied that either the young men would enlist or he'd chop the chief's hand off. Before the chief could make up his mind as to whether or not the officer was serious, the hand was gone. Enlistments soared after that, but by the time the chief had recovered, most of the young men were back. The officer had been slain on a rice-stealing foray and they'd been emboldened to wander away during the leaderless period that followed. They said that soldiering didn't appeal very much to them.

It had been a costly lesson. For a while both sides had let things drift. The Cong had contented themselves with using the Moi as guides and extracting food from the tribe. But even after the chief's anger had begun to stir again, it had been nearly two months before he had decided to do something about it. He had heard about the camp Belgard had built in the foothills; he had pored over the drawings on the leaflets Belgard's helicopters had dropped; he had pondered the messages Belgard had broadcast from his low-flying planes. At last he sent four expendable Montagnard crones down, carrying the leaflets.

Belgard had welcomed the old women warmly. He had laden them with blankets, soap, food; stuffed them with ice cream. And two days later, they were gone. Finney had been ready to call it a day at that time, but Belgard had convinced him to hold off until the week's end. Then on Sunday morning, at five o'clock, the chief led his people down the slope, across the land the Americans had terraced, over the spike-filled moat, and into the hamlet. . . .

Something weightless and noisy spattered across the roof of the tent. Belgard looked up, but the sound didn't repeat itself. "Rain," Belgard said.

The monosyllable in Rhadé signified "luck" as well as "rain." It was a happy, optimistic word, and the chief smiled and nodded. He had shown a great interest in the Khmer-type plows and the sacks of ve vang seed Belgard had imported. He had lent the authority of his presence again and again to the classes Elkins had conducted for the young Moi men in rice cultivation. He had joked them back into attending when they'd grown bored; he'd threatened them back before the boredom had soured into rebellion. Since the earliest morning of time, the Moi had picked a section of land by sorcery, slashed it, burned it, exhausted it in two or three years, and moved on. Now they were being led by a visionary, whose vision was of permanence, and it unnerved them. The centuries were flashing by too fast. There was a ribald word for fertilizer in Rhadé, but they had to create a new one for the phosphate tricalcic Belgard recommended. With straight faces they called it Long Nose Dung and pretended to be a little confused as to its origin. They grumbled loudly enough for the chief to hear, but not so loudly that he'd have any of them beaten, and the secret fact was that many, especially the young girls, found the new pace exhilarating.

A heavier tattoo struck the tent, checked itself, increased.

"I don't believe," said the chief, "that the fields will be soft enough by tomorrow to plow."

It was a question.

"I don't believe they will be," Belgard agreed. "Though perhaps by the day after?"

"Perhaps," said the chief.

"My friend," Belgard said, but then his throat tightened and he stopped, afraid to clear it for fear of coughing.

Misunderstanding, the chief forced a yawn. "Well, I'm sorry," he said, "but I have a great deal of business to attend to, and I must go now." Those were the words. The meaning had to do with the compassion of the healthy man for the injured one, with courtesy, with the refusal to demean a comrade by staying to observe his pain when there was no way to alleviate it.

"Of course," Belgard said. "I know how business can pile up. I'll follow your example, now that my pain is gone and I'm no longer sleepy." He attempted to look simultaneously martyred, dutiful, and bored.

The chief hesitated.

"I'll ask your advice," Belgard said, "in the morning. My small problems can wait."

"Well," said the chief, "if I can answer the question in a word or two—"

"It concerns my injury," Belgard said.

Feigning surprise, the chief said, "Injury?"

"I fell into a foolish trap this afternoon," Belgard told him, and went on to recount the whole story. He said that while he hadn't been badly hurt, the wound in his stomach required a kind of legerdemain that the medicine men in Saigon were more adept at than Lieutenant Dodd was. He'd decided to try their magic; the drawback was that he'd have to be away from the camp for the next few critical days, and the prospect depressed him.

After winnowing out the insignificant words, the chief repeated, "Critical," in a pensive tone.

"The child," Belgard said, "was a soldier as well as a child. He'd been told how to cry, how to pull the pin on the grenade. He was very frightened, but he remembered his lessons."

"I see."

"What other tribes live in the hills?"

"Jarai, Banar, Sedang—"

"Enemies of yours?"

"No."

"Would they fight with the Cong?"

The chief raised the stump of his right wrist.

"I'm afraid," Belgard said, "that the child may have gotten back alive. If he describes my shirt—the bars on it—the Vietminh officer will know that a captain has been wounded. He may feel that enough damage has been done so that he can risk an attack."

Presently the chief murmured, "Can you tell me, mandarin, why the Vietnamese are fighting each other?"

"I cannot," Belgard said. "I can give you some of the stated reasons."

"Please."

"Freedom. Slavery. Revenge. Power. Territory. Instinct."

The last two were the words in Rhadé for the yellowish hair-bristling rage a tiger feels at the sight of a second tiger on his preserve, and the chief whispered, "Yes, yes—" almost to himself. Then: "Mandarin, where is your home?"

"A great distance away."

"Beyond Saigon?"

"Yes."

"Why are you here?"

"The Vietnamese," Belgard said, "are cubs from the North and the South who met on the same path and asked for help. Diem's tiger is called America. Ho's is called China."

"Then those are the tigers who are really at war."

"Those are the tigers."

"The Cong officer disagreed."

"I know, but those are the tigers all the same."

"This man was Vietnamese—this officer. He felt that this is a war between colors. He told my people that mandarin Diem had invited a white python to supper and that the python was smiling and squeezing, smiling and squeezing, and that the Moi would be swallowed just as soon as the snake had digested mandarin Diem."

"Did your people believe this?"

"Some did," said the chief. "Some do."

"And what," Belgard asked, "do you believe?"

The chief reflected. "I suppose I feel that I'd rather be squeezed to death than chopped to pieces. Given a choice."

"Do you feel squeezed?"

Smiling, the chief said, "No, but then perhaps mandarin Diem hasn't been digested yet."

"Tough morsel," Belgard agreed.

The chief nodded, rubbing his stump, listening to the rain pound against the canvas. "Before I was elected Leader," he said, "I thought leading would be quite easy."

"It always appears so."

"But what terrible choices yes and no are. The auguries say one thing, the Ancestors another. . . . I would imagine that it's sometimes difficult even for your own lord Ken Ne Dy."

"On occasion," Belgard said. "I would imagine."

"Then," said the chief a little shyly, "one makes the right decision and—" The brown fingers massaged the rounded wrist in preoccupied embarrassment. "I won-

—43—

dered at first if this camp would turn into a prison. Now it seems like a cool island in the middle of a dangerous river to me." Again he paused. "My—nightmare is that *you* may consider it a prison, for yourselves—"

Belgard regarded him silently, and in a moment the chief raised his eyes. "Why do you say that?" Belgard asked.

"Do you have a mate?"

"Yes."

"Mountains of your own? Don't you ever grow home-sick?"

Belgard said, "If we left, would you stay alone here? Would you plant the fields? Could you use the guns effectively?"

"Yes," said the chief. Then: "Do you mean now?"

"In a few months."

"Yes."

"What would happen," Belgard went on, "if the Cong broke through the gates—and we had left too soon?"

"More recruiting," said the chief.

"And to you? Personally?"

"Oh—"

"The other hand?"

"They make lavish threats," said the chief. "Very colorful, but—"

"Tell me."

"They promised to disembowel my family and me. My seven-year-old son—then my wife—then myself."

"I can't believe," Belgard began, "that anyone—"

"No disemboweling in your province?" inquired the chief.

"Not of children," Belgard said, and recalled the Mississippi boy Emmett Till. "There's a pan," he said, "I think by the—"

But it was too late. Before the chief could move, Belgard's pointless retching had begun. The chief flung the tent flap open, and Dodd, who had been watching from the NCO tent nearby, came splashing and sliding back through the mud. He cradled Belgard's head in his hands. "Take a breath," he said. "Deep. Hold it. Hold it."

"I'm all right now." Drenched in sweat, swallowing, Belgard stared at the roof.

"Belly hurt?"

"Yes."

Dodd tossed the thin blanket back.

"Be careful."

"Did you bring anything up?"

"No."

"Spittle? Blood?"

"No."

"I hate to give you another shot," Dodd muttered. "What happened?"

"Nothing. I swallowed the wrong way."

Dodd rose. "I want you to go to sleep now. Say good-by to the chief in the morning."

"How do you say good-by to Emmett Till?" Belgard asked. "That's my problem."

Dodd looked down at him. "Don't think about it," he said. "I'm absolutely going to lay it on the line for you, Jack. If you start coughing or vomiting again—and that shrapnel's resting against something vital—you have had it. How do you say good-by to Cookie?"

At last Belgard said, "Leonard, did you ever have the feeling that you'd just like to turn off this piss-poor world like a light for about six months?"

"Yes," Dodd said.

"If you can't fix it, they shouldn't make you sit and look at it."

"Who says you can't fix it?"

"You're right," Belgard said. "I'll go to Finney, and I'll say, 'George, you're in error,' and he'll say, 'Oh, my God, Jack, really? *I* didn't realize that!' and I'll say, 'Oh, yes, yes, you're in error,' and he'll say, 'Well, Jesus, I'm sure sorry, but don't you worry about it, I'll send the Twenty-Fifth up there and everything's going to be just the way you want it, because after all you're a captain and a real sweet guy and I'm nothing but a damn fool major.'"

Belgard tried to suppress a strangled cough, and couldn't, and Dodd said, "Fine, keep it up." His lips were white and pinched. "I mean it," he said. "Cough yourself inside out. I'm through pleading with you." He jammed his hands into his pockets and shouldered past the chief into the rain again.

The chief seemed to bob for a moment on the waves of emotion Dodd left in his wake. Then he said, "I'm very tired, mandarin. Have I answered all your questions?"

"Yes," Belgard said.

"When do you go to Saigon?"

"Tomorrow."

"I've never been there," said the chief. "I understand it's a larger village than this, though."

"Somewhat."

"Many strangers." The chief cleared his throat. "If you're a little uneasy—if you need charms, weapons—"

"Thank you," Belgard said. "No. I'll be safe."

"Will you be concerned about the fields?"

"Concerned?"

"The young men," said the chief, "sometimes appear indifferent to the idea of the planting. They sit on their heels; they talk in class—giggle. But they'll remember it all the first time they're struck. If they don't, I'll remember it for them. I listened to every word. Plow the fields as soon as the rain has made them soft enough. Harrow. Leave the soil for two days to air—plow again—harrow again. When the rice seeds in the dampened baskets have germinated, scatter them on the seedbeds—transplant when the seedlings are this high." The chief indicated with his spread fingers.

"Exactly right," Belgard whispered.

"Good night, mandarin," said the chief.

Alone, Belgard listened to the clamorous storm and wondered if hatred could move the mountains that faith balked at. He thought of Finney dead. There was Finney gingerly perched in a helicopter groping through the night, and there was a lightning bolt pinching his head off. (He diverted the bolt from the roters to Finney's head at the last second; he wished no harm to the pilot.)

But the sport failed to console him. He needed practical plans rather than voodoo. He would be in Saigon by noon. He had gone over Finney's head before; he could try it again. He began to plot a two-pronged encirclement. He recalled a colonel on Harkins's staff named Juarez, a bull-necked propaganda-oriented man who had warned an indoctrination meeting of the absolute need to keep faith wherever it had been pledged in this tragic torn land. He would speak to Juarez. In addition, he had met a persuasive pro-Montagnard monk at the Doc Lap pagoda during his first week in Vietnam. At forty, Thich Tinh Hoa was already a venerable to be reckoned with in Buddhist circles, a sophisticate who spoke four languages and was a graduate of the Sorbonne. Dodd had reminded Belgard of a vital fact: Major Finney was only an adviser; final decisions would be made by Province Chief Tai—and Tai was a Buddhist.

Cheered, Belgard thought about the morning's trip and grew wider and wider awake. It occurred to him that he hadn't much time to waste. Finney would be in Saigon too, and Finney's mind would be clear.

He concentrated on relaxing. But there were distractions. His pillow was too hard. The cot was too short. His stomach hurt.

Cookie, as an aid to sleep, had spelled complicated words backwards. He tried "Czechoslovakia." Then he said his multiplication tables through 13 and then he became frustrated to the edge of rage attempting to remember how to discover the number of square feet in a non-equilateral triangle.

He decided to request a sedative, but after he had shouted "Dodd!" three or four times, he realized that he could never be heard over the clatter of the storm, and that Dodd probably was asleep by now in the NCO tent.

"So that's the sign," Grainger had said. "Garden. I close my eyes, I imagine a door—any kind of a door—and in the center of this door I draw the character for 'garden.' Time passes. The door opens. I walk through—" "Into a garden?" "Willow trees, fountains—" "You've hypnotized yourself."

Belgard expelled his breath and thought, *Oh, why the hell not.*

His back, he discovered, was ramrod-tense; he gaped to loosen his cheek and jaw muscles. He let his hands hang dead and concerned himself with the problem of the door.

He fussed at first over what sort of a door to imagine, but as the minutes ticked by, the question of choice grew less and less pressing because in fact he couldn't think of *any* door—not a postern, not a gate, not a mousehole, nothing. He fought this odd impotence until his skin tingled, but nothing materialized. He attempted to recall the ideograph and couldn't even do that. He became obsessed by the conceit that he was a blind, crazy old man in a state home, and that every step he'd taken to reach this particular instant had been imaginary, the result of delirium and drugs. He knew that it wasn't true, but he felt that he'd be a fool to open his eyes and *risk* having it be true. Instead, he huddled at the bottom of the uterine sea, careful not to cause the slightest wave. There he fed the fishes his fingers and arms and listened to the earth slip by on its greased axle, a comfortable grind, very soft when you considered the monstrous weight involved. A blunt-nosed shark plunged past and swam off with the end of him, a strip of forehead flesh, and it was as though a cataract had been peeled from his eye: there was the door—there was the ideograph on the door—all as ordered as a stage set. He suspected a trick, but the door withstood pressure and he was able to scrape a bit of moss from the chain that hung across it, so he was forced to accept the evidence of his senses.

He could find no knob, however, no keyhole, no bolt, no visible way to pull or push it open. It was as unattractive a door as he had ever seen. Lichens discolored the rusted hinges. The wood, particularly in the neighborhood of the Chinese sign, was pitted and putrescent; the sign itself tended to quiver and re-form and slip, and when he scrutinized it more closely he noticed to his disgust that it was composed of yellow maggots of some sort, fat feeding worms, sluggish and blind.

He also began to notice suddenly that the angle of the door was changing. He never was able to catch it in motion; it moved on his blink, no more than an inch or two at a time. Its shift was inward, away from him, and everything that lay beyond was desirable as well as dreadful, shadowed; the short hair at the nape of his neck stirred gently.

"Well, come in," someone said.

This room faced west.

"Oh, does it?" someone said. "I never noticed."

But there was no talisman over the entrance.

"Talisman?"

The octagonal thuong luong with a mirror in the center—to ward off the five demons.

"You must have made a study of these things."

No. No.

"And this is Tran Minh Chau—"

No.

She was standing in front of the Buddhist altar, enveloped in flames, groaning in pain, smiling at him in a polite, detached, dazed way. She was twenty-two years old. She was wearing an elegant white ao dai, high-collared, sheath-slim; a conical straw hat dangled by a blue chin ribbon from her slender left hand. "Why is he so frightened?" she inquired in French. Love and despair and horror left him speechless.

"Have a drink, Captain," someone said.

A breeze brushed a glass wind chime.

"I can't stay," said the girl.

"You will."

"I can't."

"You'll be back."

Her perfume was Parisian; her slanted eyes were black, her finger tips red as blood.

Outside, a monkey with a thin silver chain around its neck ran to and fro like a madman.

CHAPTER 5

THE SITUATION next day remained Normal.

By nine o'clock, it had become manifest to Dodd that no H-21 pilot, no matter how talented, was going to be able to locate the camp through the massive overcast, and accordingly he advised Ton That that it would be wiser to delay the captain's evacuation until Friday. Ton That said that was fine with them, since all their helicopters were occupied elsewhere anyway. They were both about to sign off when Grainger came into the radio shack to tell Dodd that some nut in a two-man job had just landed in a cleared patch halfway up the middle terrace.

"Whose side is he on?" Dodd asked stupidly.

"Well, ours," Grainger said. "I think."

"Arrow to Quiver," Dodd said.

"Quiver, go ahead," said Ton That.

"A chopper just dropped in on us. Did you send him?"

"No, no," said Ton That. "We canceled that. It's raining."

"*I* know it's raining," Dodd said.

"We'll try to get something to you tomorrow, O.K.?"

An Air Force lieutenant in his twenties poked his head into the shack. "Anybody home?" he asked.

"Listen, Quiver," Dodd began. "Quiver—"

"Is this man I'm going to take out ambulatory?" asked the lieutenant.

"No, sir," Grainger said. "We'll have to unbolt that extra seat, slide him in along there."

"Roger," said the lieutenant and disappeared.

"Quiver, go ahead," said Ton That.

"Never mind, Quiver," Dodd said wearily.

"Don't worry about the chopper. We'll catch him while he's circling—bring him back."

"Yeah, good," Dodd said.

"Over and out," said Ton That.

Dodd glanced at Grainger, who was biting reflectively at a hangnail. "What do you think, Sergeant?"

"Well," Grainger said, "he got *in*, sir."

Dodd nodded, gazing at the floor. At last he raised his poncho hood and headed for the door. "Sometimes I really miss the old mortuary game," he said. "Very placid trade."

CHAPTER 6

THE SKY had a convex sag to it. It bellied into the trough of the foothills like a hammock full of water, ready to split down its gross middle, Belgard thought, at any moment.

Grainger and a man from Fresno named Bagdasarian carried him out to the paddy. Dodd insisted on coming along, too—to tuck him in, he said—but Belgard bade good-by to the rest of his men at the double bamboo gate. They bunched awkwardly around his stretcher and wished him luck and told him not to take any wooden piasters. He promised he wouldn't and mentioned that he ought to be back before the middle of June. He warned them particularly to be on the alert for marauding monkeys; he said they could really wreck a new rice field.

"All right, let's go while he's still got a ceiling," Dodd said, and set off briskly through the mist. Belgard couldn't see past Bagdasarian at the foot of the stretcher, but he waved anyway, and then he fixed his gaze on the peak of Bagdasarian's poncho and tried to brace himself against the bob and bump of the ride.

The pilot had propped the door open for them. Belgard, aware for the first time of the size of the helicopter, looked at Dodd and said, "This is a gag. Isn't it?"

"It'll hold you," Dodd said.

"Me, yes—what about him?"

"I kneel on the step and pump with the other foot," said the pilot. He wore a shapeless crumpled cap and a yellow silk scarf. He took the head of the stretcher from Grainger and guided it along the floor while Bagdasarian and Dodd shoved from the outside end.

"Are you in?" Dodd yelled.

"Leonard," Belgard said, "would you do me a favor? Would you crawl underneath and push when we leave?"

Dodd chuckled and said, "Don't worry about it. Just remember that any place a helicopter can land, it can take off from again. Isn't that right, Lieutenant?"

"Not necessarily," said the pilot. He squeezed back into his seat. "Well, shall we give her a go?" he asked.

"Jesus God," Belgard said. "I've felt doomed before, but this is ridiculous. Leonard?"

"We won't leave you," Dodd reassured him. "We'll all be right down here, cheering."

"Well, thank you, sports fans," Belgard said.

He felt a hand on his shin, and then he heard Dodd say, "Good-by, Jack," and he raised his own hand and waved. The pilot leaned across him and pulled the door shut. "*Here* we go," he said.

But almost at once there was a pounding on the door, and the pilot had to lean back and reopen it.

"Who's that?" Belgard called. "What's the matter?"

"You almost forgot your game, Captain," Grainger answered.

"Keep it, I don't want the damn—" But Grainger had already wedged the cylinder between Belgard's feet and his duffel bag. Again the pilot banged the door shut.

There was a series of embarrassed little farts from the motor; the overhead blades flapped and shook.

"I hope my baggage isn't too heavy for you," Belgard shouted. "Have you ever carried this much extra baggage before?"

"I've never carried an extra *man* before," the pilot shouted back. "This is a Courier—for messages."

"Let me out," Belgard shouted. "I've changed my mind."

The gummy earth sucked at the wheels; the light frame shivered. The only prayer Belgard could think of was Now I Lay Me Down to Sleep.

Straining, they broke free of the grip of the mud and went wallowing through the torpid air like one of Dracula's lesser bats.

" 'Off we go,' " the pilot sang, " 'into the wild blue yonder—' "

CHAPTER 7

THE AIRPORT at Ton That was situated in a grove of pine trees near the eastern end of an emerald-colored lake. By the time Belgard's chopper landed, the rain had stopped and the air was fresh and cool. A detail led by an emaciated sergeant transported his stretcher directly to a waiting C-47. Everyone moved at a half-gallop; the plane was ready at the end of its runway, motors roaring. Deafened, breathless, Belgard was lashed into place, the detail tumbled out in harried disorder, someone beyond Belgard's line of vision slammed and bolted the door closed, and the pilot cut his engines off.

After a ten-minute wait, they taxied back to what Belgard presumed was the plane's hardstand, and, so far as Belgard could tell, everybody filed out of the plane and went home.

It took twenty-five minutes more for him to explode.

He began to pound flat-handed on the inner wall by his head, and then he located the Chinese game and used the metal end of that, and forty-six minutes after he had been plummeted across the field and into the C-47, a

Korean mechanic looked in and asked him who he was and what he thought he was doing.

Belgard told him.

The mechanic brought the copilot on the run.

"Now what seems to be the trouble, buddy," the co-pilot began.

"What's your rank, buddy?"

"Lieutenant."

"You address me as 'sir,' Mister, or I'll climb off this fucking bunk if it's the last move I make on earth and I'll cut your fucking head off *and stuff it up your fucking ass!* DO YOU READ ME?"

"Yes, sir!" said the lieutenant.

"NOW WHO'S IN CHARGE OF THIS LUMBER-ING PIECE OF JUNK?"

"Captain Swanson, sir!"

"AND WHERE IS CAPTAIN SWANSON?"

"Right outside, sir—I'll get him!"

Captain Swanson resembled an extremely small John Wayne. He had Mississippi-basin cheekbones and a severe cold. Belgard considered him a mortal enemy on sight.

"Sir," said Captain Swanson in the hoarsest, kindest voice Belgard had ever heard, "I'm deeply sorry for this tedious delay, and I apologize for the incomprehensible rudeness with which you've been treated. If there is any way I can make up for it, I am at your command, believe me. May I fetch you some coffee?"

Belgard closed his mouth. "No," he said.

"Copy of the post newspaper?"

"Thank you no."

"I was under the impression," said Captain Swanson, "that you had been told what happened. That's one of my biggest failin's. I sometimes give an order and then become so involved in outside details that I neglect to check back."

"Well, you can't do everything yourself, Captain," Belgard said.

"No, sir, but it's a matter of relative importance. I've flown wounded men into Saigon before, and I will not tolerate soldiers in pain bein' treated like sides of beef."

"Well, actually," Belgard said, "I was more confused than anything. I thought we were all ready to take off when I came aboard—"

"So did I," said Captain Swanson, "and I've been fightin' with the control tower about it ever since."

"What's the delay?"

"Another passenger—"

"Swannie?" The lieutenant called from the door, and Swanson looked back and then rose.

"Here he is," he said to Belgard. "Again—I'm sorry. We'll get you there as soon as we can. I've asked Tan Son Nhut to have an ambulance standin' by for you." He smiled, and sidled past the new passenger. "Welcome aboard, Major," he said.

"Where do I sit," Belgard heard Finney ask, "any place?"

CHAPTER 8

AT FORTY-EIGHT, George Finney reminded Belgard of a miler who had inexplicably forgotten that he'd been lapped. He continued to run with grace and cunning, unaware that the cheers were for the men behind him.

He was six feet tall, clear-eyed and black-haired, too handsome to be an actor and probably too honest to be a politician, although it was Belgard's understanding that he'd shone at both trades in school. He was married to an heiress, played tennis like a champion, had three intelligent children, and had been a major since Korea, which indicated to everyone but Finney that his army career was over. The unquenchable inner strength that ought to have made him a tragic figure irritated his men instead and baffled his superiors. It had a dishonest ring to it, as if Finney had elected to martyr himself in a safe cause.

During their slow taxi back to the head of the runway, he insisted on apologizing for the delay at such length and in so candid a manner that even before their wheels left the ground he had driven Belgard close to insanity from suppressed fury. He took the entire blame on his shoulders. He had two passions, he said, polo and hunting, and while he never expected to hear the good chunk of mallet on ball until he had regained civilization, he had made up his mind to sneak in a little hunting, at least, whenever he could. He supposed Belgard preferred the swifter game—panther, stag—but he, personally, was a bear man.

"I don't hunt," Belgard said.

"What do you mean, you don't hunt?"

"I mean I don't hunt."

"Nothing at all?"

"Nothing at all."

"You fish, though."

"No."

"That's really difficult for me to understand," Finney said. "I've never been able to get it out of my head that there was something a little—I don't know—effeminate, about a man who doesn't fish or hunt. Present company excepted, of course."

"Of course," Belgard said.

"I know it is an unfair evaluation, but I can't seem to help it."

"Well, we all have our little hang-ups," Belgard said.

"At any rate," Finney went on, "I've made it a point ever since I was assigned to this area to hunt on Thursdays. Thursday is Hunt Day for me up here."

"Ah," said Belgard.

"I'm generally back by eight-thirty or nine, but I couldn't break it off today for some reason. I don't mean I'd forgotten about you. I remembered you were due in."

"You should have told me about Hunt Day," Belgard said. "I could have waited over."

"Heart-rending." Finney laughed. "Come on now, let's not be pitiable, please."

"God forbid." Belgard chuckled.

"No, I goofed," Finney said. "I should have come back sooner."

"Or assigned two planes," Belgard said.

"Why?" Finney asked. "Did the delay bother you that much?"

"No, no," Belgard said.

"Well, I'm certainly sorry," Finney said. He studied Belgard in amused contempt for a second and then turned his head to gaze out the window. "Where'd you get it, by the way?" he asked, turning back.

"Oh, here and there," Belgard said thickly. "legs, belly—"

"This was an ambush? On patrol?"

"More or less."

"Booby trap?"

"Grenade."

"You ran into a VC group, then."

"No, Montagnard—"

"Are you sure?" Finney asked.

"Certainly I'm sure. Why? They're not all loyal to us."

"Oh, I don't think any of them are loyal," Finney said. "Or *dis*loyal. They're children. It's just that a grenade's a very sophisticated instrument for a Montagnard to use."

"Major—"

"All right, Jack. I know where you stand on these people—you know where I stand—let's not argue about it."

"I'm not arguing—"

"Even the Vietnamese can't swallow the Moi, Jack, you know that as well as I do. Don't tell me about the Moi. I've had the Moi up to here." Finney fell silent, brooding. "Let me tell you something. I've hunted all over the world, and I've had some fair guides and I've had some bad ones, but I've never had any worse bearers than these idiots. If you think the American nigger's retarded, you ought to have my job for a day or two."

"Listen—"

"You can bleed for them, you can try to educate them, you can tax the white workingman out of existence pandering to them, but Jack, you cannot change the shape of the skull or the size of the brain, and you know that as well as I know it. And your average Montagnard isn't even up to the capabilities of your average nigger. I mean, I've seen plenty of niggers in this man's army who make pretty good soldiers and so have you. Will you admit that, at least?"

"I'll admit that," Belgard said hoarsely. "I'll admit more—"

"Just let me finish," Finney said, "and then you can climb up on your soapbox. I have felt for years and years that there is nothing more perilous on this earth than the Red Menace. I have watched more and more of this globe eaten away, and I tell you unequivocally that if we don't stop it here we ain't gonna *stop* it!"

"The way to stop it," said Belgard, "is to recognize that the Communists appeal to certain people by appearing to *care* about—"

"Oh, *horse* manure!" Finney said. "The way to stop it is to quit all this snatch-grabbin' and pitch the Bomb right down their goddam throats! I could cry when I see the greatest country on earth handcuffed by a bunch of pricks that call themselves the U.N.—"

"The *Bomb!*"

"The Bomb! Certainly the Bomb! What the hell have we got it for? What side is that pinko bastard in the

White House *on?* Who crucified General Walker? You going to tell me that wasn't a direct order from Rome?"

"From *who* in Rome? That pinko egghead Commie dupe in the Vatican?! Major, for Christ's sake—"

"You bet your goddam rock-bottom mother-lovin' *dollar* that Commie in the Vatican! There is a hot line *direct* from—"

"Major, Major—"

"There is a *hot* line direct from Vatican *City* to Washington, and *you* are gonna wake up to it just about the time Vincent Cardinal Sheeney is made Secretary of *State*, my friend! What is the *matter* with Americans? My God, how loud does the tocsin have to be sounded? There is at this minute a *Russian* commanding an American army at a base in the South; right now there is I don't know how many yellow Chinese troops on the Mexican-American border—don't shake your head at me; read the bulletins! God's abdicated, Buster, I believe it, or lightning would have struck 'em all by now—that traitor in the White House, those Commies on the Supreme Court —struck 'em *down*, struck 'em *dead*—"

He broke off to stare out at the clouds below the port wing. A vein pumped in his neck. He lifted a finger and wiped the bubbles away from the corner of his mouth.

"I was of course speaking metaphorically," he said.

Belgard failed to answer, and Finney looked at him intently for a moment, then returned his gaze to the wing.

It wasn't until they were over the airport that Finney reopened his mouth. "Too bad about Colonel Juarez, wasn't it?" he said.

"Juarez?"

"Did you know him?"

"Well, I know who he is," Belgard said.

"Was," Finney said. "He was killed Wednesday."

He presented his athlete's back and watched the runways of Tan Son Nhut swell larger and larger in the window and never again spoke a single word to Belgard, not even "good-by."

CHAPTER 9

MERCY HOSPITAL, situated in the northeast at the far end of Thong Nhut Boulevard, had been designed originally as a small clinic for the wives and children of the Americans stationed in Saigon—the embassy staff, C.I.A. and U.S.I.S. officers, and correspondents accredited to the Gia Long Palace. Since its primary function was to reassure, there had been very little attention paid to medical convenience. The one operating arena was cramped and cheerful; a frieze of wild beasts circled its four walls at child's-eye level. There were no wards. Each miniature private room had a theme and a view. Belgard's overlooked the Botanical Gardens and had pictures of Pinocchio and the Blue Fairy drawn in pastels on the ceiling.

"We had you booked into Never-Never-Land first," Belgard's nurse told him, "but a chicken colonel with the piles beat you out." The nurse's name was Bobbie and she was from Topeka. She was compact and cute and blonde, snub-nosed. "This isn't bad, though. I mean, if you like fairies."

"Some of my best friends are fairies," Belgard said. "I just wouldn't want my sister to marry one."

"Right," Bobbie said. She located the vein she was

after and tied a stiff yellow rubber band around his upper arm. "Make a fist." The needle popped in. "O.K."

"Tell me," Belgard said, "do you know a Colonel Juarez, by any chance?"

"Juarez," Bobbie repeated. "No . . . Patient?"

"Well, I doubt it. I'm not sure. He's on Harkins's staff. I heard he'd been killed Wednesday, but the man who told me gets his kicks in some strange ways and he might have been lying."

"Oh, gee, wait a second," Bobbie said. "Wednesday?"

"Is it true?"

"Were you close?"

"No," Belgard said. "No, I'd met him once—liked him—"

"Somebody tossed a plastique into the Continental terrace. It hit his table."

Belgard studied the sad smile on the Blue Fairy's face.

"I'm terribly sorry," Bobbie said. She paused near the door and then returned to the bed. "The doctor wanted you to rest for a while before he sees you, so we weren't going to give you your mail until later, but I can tell him you wormed it out of me."

Belgard wrinkled his forehead. "Mail? Here?"

"How about that for service?" She plucked an envelope out of her pocket and held it to her nose. "Who do you know that uses Joy?"

"What's Joy?" Belgard asked.

"Joy?" Bobbie repeated blankly. "You're putting me on. You call yourself a boulevardier, and you don't know what Joy is?"

"No, I call myself a clod," Belgard said. "What's Joy?"

"Well, for your information, sonny, Joy just happens to be the world's absolutely number one perfume, that's all."

She handed him the letter, and he saw that the handwriting and the return address were Cookie's. The envelope smelled of shy colorful flowers and spring hillsides. "Delicious," he said.

"She's either terribly lonesome," Bobbie said, "or terribly friendly."

"Or both," Belgard said.

"Is our affair already doomed, Captain?" Bobbie asked. "Are you married? Is that from your wife?"

"That's who it's from," Belgard said.

"Well, back to the old bedpans." Bobbie sighed and opened the door.

"Listen, could you do me another favor?" Belgard asked.

"Sure."

"I'd like to get in touch with a Buddhist monk, a friend of mine. Could you call the Doc Lap pagoda and leave word for Thich Tinh Hoa that I'm here in—"

"Wait, wait, wait, wait," Bobbie said. "Gevalt." She fished a pad and pencil stub out of her skirt pocket. "*Thich?*"

"Three words," Belgard said, "T-H-I-C-H."

"Yeah—"

"T-I-N—as in Nellie—H."

"Yeah—"

"H-O-A. Thich Tinh Hoa."

"O.K."

"And have them tell him that I'm here in the hospital and that I've got to see him—imperative—life and death. Tell him it's about the Montagnards up around Ton That."

"Can these fellows speak English? Because I think Vietnamese is just as musical as it can be, but—"

"Tinh Hoa speaks English."

Bobbie stuffed the pad back into her pocket. "Now read your letter and try to rest. As soon as you're asleep we'll come whanging in to wake you up and give you a nice sedative." She vanished as though a hook had whipped her offstage; the door sighed shut.

Belgard sniffed at the spring flowers again and recalled the delayed honeymoon he and Cookie had had in Paris— the grave little French children in the Luxembourg in the April rain; breakfasts at Pam-Pam; Cookie's conviction that the Eiffel Tower would never support their weight. He tore the letter open and glanced first at the end of it to see the invariable "Love, Cookie." The words, in the familiar hand, were "All best wishes, Constance."

Belgard thought about that for a moment and then turned the single page over.

"Dear Jack," the letter began.

Belgard lowered the page and looked out at the entrance to the Botanical Gardens. On one side stood the National Museum; on the other was a smaller building in traditional style called the Temple de Souvenir Vietnamien. It had never, so far as he knew, been open; its purpose appeared to be purely decorative. Intrigued by its air of mischief and mystery, he had tried several times, when he was on leave, to get in but had been forced, finally, to give up.

He raised the letter again, and this time he read it through to the end.

Dear Jack,
    Rather than have you hear the news from your family or some of our so-called friends, Freddie and I decided that it would hurt you far less to hear it first from me, and our concern, honestly, is for you, believe it or not, though I know you won't and can't. Jack, I have met a wonderful man. You don't know him, but if you did, I know you would love him

as I do. He is so sweet, and he's had such a terrible life. We have sat and cried together night after night and I know he needs me as you never did. Jack, I would rather go through hell than give you an instant's pain, but I never did love you, you must have sensed that. I realized a week after the ceremony that our marriage was a farce, but I was just a silly girl then and I didn't know what true love was. Of course you'll be flooded with "helpful" mail from our so-called "friends" but just remember this, whatever Freddie and I have done, it wasn't sordid to us, it was beautiful. I told mother that I was coming up here to Vegas just for the week end, but I'm going to stay to establish residence, Jack. Freddie wasn't sure that we should hurt you by rushing a divorce through, but I know I love him, and he loves me, and that's it. If you have any regard left for me at all, you won't fight me on this. I have thought it out for several days and I know what I want. My lawyer's name is Felix Fisher, and he's in the Fidelity Building here in Las Vegas, if you should want to contact him. You won't have to appear. I believe they have a man stand in for you. We don't expect you to understand right away. If you have any questions, don't hesitate to write and ask. This may seem like a blow now, but you will find true love someday, too, as I have. That's all Freddie and I want, your happiness.

I hope you're out of the War Zone. Take care of yourself.

All best wishes
Constance

His first reaction was so low-keyed, murderous, and illogical that his mind seemed scarcely to be working at all. His heart had slowed to a snail's pace; his finger tips were numb and chilly. He was obsessed by trivial questions. He went over and over the problem of how best to trick Cookie's Las Vegas address out of the lawyer, Fisher, without alarming him. (He foresaw no awkwardness at all in *getting* to Las Vegas; there were flights out of Saigon every day, and he'd be due for a medical leave.) What he was after, he came to realize, was Crying

Freddie. It never occurred to him that Crying Freddie might be somewhere else; Cookie's capacity for self-destruction was matched only by her passion for ownership.

He thought that after he'd cut Crying Freddie's balls off to give him something legitimate to cry over, he might attempt to reason with Cookie.

But reason with her, he wondered, about what? The lack of sportsmanship she was showing in holding a back-alley tomcat to a promise of engagement? The sad cheapness involved in romanticizing a squeaking motel bed?

He filled his lungs and reread the latter, and only then —the second time through—was he able to grasp its sadism fully. The words were a parody of a thoughtless child's. Cookie never had done anything in a gush of emotion, although that was part of her legend. Belgard lowered the scented paper to his chest and considered the corrosive hatred that had motivated this grotesque act of adultery, and he thought, *My God, where was I when the pool of acid was building?* He had loved her. He had thought he'd loved her. He'd known her most of his life, but obviously he had loved something else. And what kind of a masochist was he to have tolerated and abetted it all? The roots of infidelity were too complex to be whimsical; Crying Freddie couldn't have been the first to cuckold him, even if he had been the first physically. The problem was deeper than the illegitimate squirming of his wife on a borrowed bed grunting up at a bug-eyed cozener that she had at last found true love. The wedding vows had been broken by whichever of them had initially realized that there was no respect in it and had said nothing. Himself? Cookie? Both of them? That, it seemed to Belgard, was the most wicked part of the plot. There were ways and ways to end a marriage. This—from the form of it to the timing—struck him as the maddest. He realized how little he knew about his wife; he expected, however, that she would be astounded to learn that he considered himself the injured party. She had, after all, told him. It wasn't as though she had kept her itch for Crying Freddie secret the way a great many inconsiderate girls might have.

He lay as still as he could and built his wall brick by brick against the intolerable pain of this rejection. To stuff the chinks, he used whatever material was at hand, from rage to rationalization, though fact continued to seep through, no matter what he chose. *I never did love you, you must have sensed that.* Had he? Was it possible that the Mark always connived with the Swindler to bring the fraud about?

The blood-swollen cells of his brain wouldn't work. There was no comfort short of slaughter here, except in flight. So he ran like Charlie Chaplin from the bullet-helmeted police, up hill and down dale, dwindling to a comic pinpoint, irising out just before The End appeared on the screen.

CHAPTER 10

THE DOOR was clearer this time, far less dreamlike. It hung askew on its rotted hinges, half drowned in moss and undergrowth. It opened before he touched it; it seemed to shrink away from his finger tips like appalled belly flesh. There were barbaric sounds in the air, odors of jasmine and joss. Something said to him that if he stopped right now he would be less than hooked. He would never be the same, but he would not be destroyed.

He walked into a courtyard crowded with old women in black pajamas and bald saffron-robed monks. A boy scout said in tortured English, "Americans—Number Ten," and spat in his face. Two slender Vietnamese girls covered their mouths and giggled as he passed.

He shouldered the hostile jostling beggars aside; if he'd had a club he'd have used it. On the crumbling pagoda steps, under a profusion of Buddhist flags, stood a tiny nun. She smiled tenderly at him through betel-blackened teeth and pressed a soiled paper tract into his hands. "Youth of Vietnam," it read, "be ready to sacrifice yourself for Buddha and drive the Americans into the sea."

"Bonjour, mon vieux," someone said.

He looked up toward the jagged peaks of the pagoda scratched against the sky. On the second-floor balcony, Thich Tinh Hoa fingered his amber beads, a tall frail man enveloped in a gray robe. The bones of his face and shaven head were as tense and delicate as crystal. "What do you want, Captain?" he asked.

"You were expecting me, Tinh Hoa," Belgard said. "Don't ask ridiculous questions."

"Very well, then," Tinh Hoa said. "The girl called. But she said you were in the hospital."

"You see that I'm not."

"You're a very sick man, Captain. You ought not to be out of bed."

"I'm coming up."

"Why?"

"You know why. The letter. Why did you betray me, Tinh Hoa?"

"What letter? Betray you how?"

Belgard started past the tiny nun, and at the same time a young monk smelling of onions grabbed him from behind and pinned his arms to his sides. He jackknifed forward. The monk's feet stumbled against the stone steps; the large peasant backside slapped the ground heavily.

Thich Tinh Hoa shouted an order down in Vietnamese, but it was too late. Grease shone on a blunt dagger the young monk had dug out of his orange sleeve.

"Use it," Belgard whispered in French. "Try."

The monk's black eyes remained fixed on his. Wind rustled through the torn paper banners pasted to the stucco walls. On the fringes of the crowd, children demanded explanations in piping voices.

The monk lifted himself like a snake, straight upward, mute, barely swaying.

Thich Tinh Hoa repeated his strident order.

"They'll think you're afraid," Belgard whispered. "Try."

The point of the knife touched Belgard's chest.

"Do you understand what I'm going to do?" Belgard continued. "I'm going to snap his neck like the stem of a flower. You could stop it, coward—"

The dagger shot forward; Belgard sank back and gripped the wrist, corkscrewing the monk across the fulcrum of his leg. Spectators scattered. The monk landed on his stomach and rolled over, eyes to the sky, both arms broken. A pedicab driver drew the saffron skirt chastely over the bleeding knees.

Thich Tinh Hoa hadn't moved by the time Belgard reached the balcony. People poured through the iron-grill gate into the courtyard below, ants converging in greedy anxiety on a broken orange honeypot.

"I think you're insane," Tinh Hoa said. "Let me call a doctor." It had begun to rain a little; dark spots appeared here and there on the gray robe. "Come inside—"

"I want to know why you betrayed me."

"Yes, let's talk about it in the reception room. I have a soft sofa for you to lie on." He placed his arm around Belgard's shoulders. "Now what's all this about a letter?"

"She didn't tell you?"

"All she said was something about the Montagnards near Ton That—"

It was raining harder now, but he continued to resist Thich Tinh Hoa's efforts to lead him inside. Over the tap of the rain on the wooden overhang, he thought he could hear a siren. He walked to the edge of the balcony. An American Army patrol wagon nosed through the press of people at the main gate. A wave of nausea overtook him; he caught hold of the iron railing and hung on until his dizziness passed.

"Come along, Captain," Tinh Hoa wheedled. "Come inside, mon cher, hm?" Skeletal fingers plucked at the cuff of his jacket. The skin over the long bones was pale and translucent. Turning, Belgard picked up Tinh Hoa and bent him over the low railing. Tinh Hoa had begun to shriek. The hem of the gray robe caught on a sharp splinter of wood; Belgard kicked it free and stuffed the witless struggling man over the edge of the balcony into the rain. The gray bundle fluttered toward the scampering figures below, struck the courtyard head first. Belgard was certain he could hear the distinct crack of the neck. Watery blood reddened the pool of water Tinh Hoa lay in.

"Murder!" someone kept screaming in Vietnamese.

CHAPTER 11

"CAPTAIN," whispered the nurse, "no, no—it's all right—look here, look—"

"But you can't mistake a sound like that," Belgard whispered back. "It was his neck. The man's dead."

"Where are you?"

"What?"

The nurse moved her blonde head aside. "Look at the ceiling. Do you remember the fairy?"

The Disneyish drawing regarded him compassionately out of wide doe eyes. Nearby, Pinocchio despaired over the length of his nose.

"When you have a bad dream, boy," Bobbie said, "you don't mess around, do you?"

Cookie's letter had slipped to the floor. The nurse retrieved it and placed it next to the Chinese game on his night stand. The top of the cylinder had been removed; Belgard's wand lay beside it, behind a bubble-coated glass of water. Refraction thickened and magnified the ideograph.

"Hey, what's this?" Bobbie asked.

Belgard said, "That's a game." Everything in him ached —every muscle, every atom.

"How do you play it?"

"You don't," Belgard said. "It plays you."

Bobbie laughed politely and said, "Oh, I called your friend."

"Was he there?"

"Well, he was at the pagoda, but they said he was on the balcony, talking to some American Army captain, and he'd have to contact you later."

Belgard's blinds had been lowered. "Is it raining?" he whispered.

"Yes, why?"

"No reason."

"Not hard, but at least it'll settle the dust."

"Good."

"How do you feel?"

"I'm not a mystic," Belgard answered. "I don't believe in it; Grainger does, but I don't. Don't talk to me about the Mysterious East."

"O.K., I won't," Bobbie said, but her voice had grown persuasive and gentle again.

"I'm all right," Belgard told her. "I got some news that shook me up, but I'm not wandering. I'm in Mercy Hospital in Saigon. Grainger's a sergeant of mine."

"And you feel peculiar because you had some kind of a mystic experience?"

"I don't know what I had. I had a very realistic dream."

"Yeah, they can sure fog you up, can't they?" Bobbie said.

"I know what happened," Belgard said. "I wanted to kill somebody, so I killed somebody in my nightmare. I've just never had one as real as that."

"Listen, better you should kill 'em in a dream," Bobbie said. "They hang you for murder in this man's army."

"So they do."

"Who'd you kill?"

"My friend. Tinh Hoa."

"Positively no sweat," Bobbie said. "I'll testify you were flat on your back in bed during the whole squalid affair. It was this other nut who *looked* like you."

The door opened and a middle-aged major gazed vaguely in. "Who's this?" he asked Bobbie.

"This is Captain Belgard, Doctor," Bobbie said.

"Who?"

"Belgard," Belgard said.

"Uh huh," said the major and left.

Belgard met Bobbie's eyes, and Bobbie said reassuringly, "He'll remember you on the table. He always says he never forgets a wound."

"Or a bad joke," Belgard said.

"Or a bad joke."

"Will you raise those blinds?" Belgard asked.

Bobbie crossed to the window and lifted the blind. The trees in the courtyard were gleaming and motionless.

"There's absolutely no way, is there," Belgard said, "that I could have gotten out of this room?"

"I'll tell you what I think I'll do," Bobbie said. "Why don't I call your friend again, and when I get him on the line, I'll bring a phone in here and have him switched over. Would you know his voice?"

Belgard nodded.

"O.K., you relax for a second," Bobbie said. She smiled and started away, and then stood aside as the middle-aged major returned. He was carrying several large X rays. He paused at the foot of Belgard's bed, absorbed in the plates. Bobbie waited for a decent interval, then mouthed, "I'll be right back," and slipped out of the room.

The silence lengthened. Belgard closed his lids and there the door was already gaping, and he snapped his eyes open again and glued them onto the Blue Fairy's face.

"Do you read X rays?" asked the major.

"No—"

The major sat on the side of his bed and held the pictures for him to view. "There's the splinter that's been causing you the pain."

"I see."

"Who cleaned out your leg?"

"My field medic."

"Good thorough job. You'll have some bad scars, but he got all the important shrapnel."

"When can I return to my command?"

"Oh, thirty days—"

"Hospitalized all that time?"

"No, we'll kick you out of here in two weeks or less. We'll operate tomorrow; you'll be up the next day."

The Nurse re-entered the room. Her face was expressionless; she hadn't brought the phone she'd promised.

The major slapped his knee and rose. "So O.K.," he said, "I'll see you tomorrow morning at six, Captain—?"

"Belgard," Belgard said.

"Belgard. I'm lousy with names. Forgive me. But don't worry. I never forget a wound." He left, chuckling.

Belgard hadn't taken his eyes off the nurse.

At last Bobbie said, "Did you ever run into a coincidence you couldn't explain?"

"What happened?" Belgard asked softly.

"I called the pagoda—"

"And they told you he was dead. They said he'd fallen off the balcony."

Bobbie peered at him. "Dead? Why, no. Dead?"

"Where is he, then?"

"Well, he's right here," Bobbie said. "That's the coincidence."

"I—don't—"

"I walked down to the main desk, and I picked up the phone, and I noticed this Vietnamese monk talking to the girl on duty, but—I don't know—for some reason it just didn't register. Anyway, when I got the pagoda, I asked for Thich Tinh Hoa, and the monk right there— right beside me—turned, and he said, 'Yes?'—you know —and I *looked* at him, I was still talking into the phone, and I said 'Are *you* Reverend Hoa?' and he said, '*Yes, who are you?*' and I said, well, I was calling for Captain Belgard, and he said he was *looking* for Captain Belgard, and all this time this poor fellow on the other end of the line thought I was talking to him and he kept trying to answer me, and we all got to laughing—"

"Well," Belgard began, "you mean, he'd gotten your message—"

"*No*," Bobbie said. "Well, he'd gotten a message that you were in the *hospital*, but apparently somebody else had told him." She shook her head. "*I* don't know—he can explain it better than I can. He's outside. Do you want to see him?" She pushed the door ajar. "Reverend Hoa?"

She left the room as Tinh Hoa entered. The unharmed shaven head atop the slender neck bowed over the joined finger tips, and then the right hand was clasping Belgard's warmly. "Comment ça va, mon vieux? I was sorry—so very sorry—to hear of this accident. I pray it's not serious."

"Thank you, no—it isn't."

"My friend Tai contacted me this morning. The province chief."

"Yes—"

"And he said that you'd been wounded." Tinh Hoa drew a straight-back chair to the bed and sat down, settling the saffron robe around him. "He seemed to take it as a personal affront on Fate's part. He's afraid you won't be coming back." Tinh Hoa paused. "He asked me to sound you out. He told me to approach you with the greatest circumspection, to be extremely discreet—subtle as the serpent—"

"Oriental," Belgard suggested.

"Exactly. He said Americans expected that."

"Always."

"Well? Will you be coming back?"

"Yes."

"Let's not fence with each other, Captain," Tinh Hoa said sternly, and Belgard laughed for the first time in what seemed to be weeks. Smiling, Tinh Hoa added, "Then I can tell him you do plan to extend—"

"Yes. Who told him I didn't?"

"I'm not sure. Would there be someone named Finney up there?"

"There would."

Tinh Hoa nodded.

"You reassure me in a way," Belgard said.

"Indeed?"

"Any officer who takes a stand on his own takes it primarily in the dark. It helps to know Tai shares my point of view."

"*Our* point of view," Tinh Hoa said. "You're speaking of the Montagnards?"

"I think," Belgard said, "there must have been more subtlety than this on the American frontier. All right. The Montagnards."

"Subtlety, it seems to me, is the province of the advocates in their capes and wigs. The trial's over for South Vietnam. The blade's already halfway down the guillotine. I don't want my country's head to fall in Ho's basket, Captain."

"And you think it might? Without the Montagnards?"

"I think it might without the help of a number of allies the Vietnamese tend to feel—conflict over. The Montagnards. President Diem. The Americans—"

Belgard watched him silently.

"Let me see if I can clarify it a little," Tinh Hoa said. He flexed his thin fists pensively. "Imagine, if you can, that the Canadians have a fully equipped guerrilla army in the United States, and that they are arming the Indians against you, and that your President is a fascist who has called on the Japanese for help. . . . Wouldn't you experience a certain inner confusion?"

"Yes."

"So you would say, 'All right, I'm in love with this country and I will focus on its first problems first. I will fight the Canadians wherever I can find them. I will arm the Indians myself. I will cooperate with the Japanese officers—especially with those who love my country, too —and I will deal with my stone-age President when my main war is won.' Entendu?"

"Bien entendu."

Tinh Hoa shrugged. "Ergo: of course Colonel Tai shares your concern. Of course he wants you back. Your camp is important to Ton That Province—to the Montagnards—to him—to all of us."

"You understand," Belgard said, "that Major Finney doesn't agree."

"How much power does Major Finney possess?"

"More than I do."

"Friends in high places?"

"I don't know."

"Would he close the camp if he could?"

"Yes."

"Is he a Communist?"

—82—

Belgard thought about Finney's scarecrows—the Pope; the scowling yellow hordes poised along the Mexican border—and said, "My God, no."

"Can you be sure?"

"I can be sure."

"Closing the camp would help the Cong. He sees that."

"No."

"Sometimes I don't believe I understand the Occidental mind," Tinh Hoa said. "What does he want?"

"Part of what you want," Belgard answered. "American withdrawal."

"What I want," Tinh Hoa said, "is to retire to a pagoda beside a placid pool and reflect on the way of Lord Buddha."

"Some day," Belgard said.

"I wonder. One grows discouraged."

"Because one grows tired. The problems never end." Belgard gazed at the Chinese stick on the night table. "The problems pile up and pile up until something snaps."

"Yes, I've seen that happen in the fuse box at Doc Lap."

"Very similar."

"I've often thought that that was probably why man devised holidays. To replace the fuse."

"Probably."

"Captain," Tinh Hoa resumed, "the war won't end on May eighth, but if you'd care to come to Hué with me, perhaps we could both find a second wind—a new fuse."

"May eighth?"

"The two thousand five hundred and seventh birthday of Lord Buddha. There'll be speeches, parades. Do you know Hué?"

"No."

"Charming city—on the River of Perfumes—more contemplative than Saigon, slower moving. I was born there. I could show you the imperial citadel, the tombs of the emperors. Gia Long himself is buried near Thien Tho mountain beside his first empress. . . . What do you say?"

"In America," Belgard said, "when a baseball game has to be postponed on account of bad weather, the management issues a rain check. I won't be out of the hospital by the eighth, but I'd like very much to see Hué later on—"

"If I'd give you a rain check on the invitation?"

"Yes."

"You have it." Tinh Hoa beamed. "Rain check. What a courteous idea. Very Asiatic. All right. Let me see. When *will* you be on your feet again?"

"Two weeks from tomorrow. Then I'll have two more free weeks before I go back to Ton That."

"Excellent. We'll fly up as soon as you're able."

"Meanwhile," Belgard said, "back at the ranch, Major Finney continues to forward his foul plans."

"Back at the—?"

"Another American cliché. It means that the villains in American cowboy pictures never sleep."

"The villains never sleep anywhere, my dear friend." Tinh Hoa sat back, musing. "Buddhists aren't exactly met with open arms by Diem and his Catholic generals, but there are a few government leaders I can talk to. . . . We'll save the camp. And then of course you must have some friends at your own court—"

"That," Belgard replied, "is one of my fuse-blowing problems."

"I don't understand."

"The man I was counting on has been killed."

"Ah," Tinh Hoa murmured. "Terrible. The deaths— the deaths. This was an American? An officer?"

"Yes."

"Killed in action?"

"In Saigon. A plastique. His name was Juarez. You may have met him."

"No."

"A very good—" He heard the crack in his own voice and paused to clear it. Tinh Hoa, he noticed, was regarding him strangely, a reaction that angered and embarrassed him for some reason. "He wasn't a friend. I barely—" The room swayed and wavered; tears scalded his eyes. "My God," he said, "what's—"

"Let it go, let it go," Tinh Hoa muttered. "Tu as raison, mon vieux. Pleure."

Belgard was two men, simultaneously stretched on the short hospital bed and seated in the audience, chief performer as well as principal critic at his own tragedy, unable either to stop or turn away. The tears flooded out. His chest was crushed by sorrow he couldn't begin to understand. "I must be crazy—"

"Or human."

"But—"

"No, it's a waste of time to argue with creation. Go back to the first man and tell him that emotion dismays you—tell him to disregard pain, to be absolutely unselfish, to bear all frustration with saintly patience—but please don't tell it to yourself and expect a reasoned answer. You're several hundred thousand years too late."

"I'm not crying for Juarez."

"Nor the camp, nor your wounds, nor your uneasiness over an operation. Not for any one thing, mon vieux; for all of it—*all* of it—for fatigue, I think, loneliness, for the war, probably for pains that are none of my business. We were talking of fuses, were we not? Don't deride weeping, or rage, or day dreams, or nightmares. How could we bear the overloads without them? It's not nice to commit murder when one finds one's wife, say, in another man's arms. It may be desirable—but, really, it's not nice at all. I speak figuratively, of course. Don't imagine a new and unnecessary problem. You have enough to serve. Are you married?"

Belgard thought about it and then shook his head.

"Much the best—in a war. Now do I have to remind you, my good friend, that Saigon is a city filled with agreeable companions? I sound, I know, like a Parisian procurer, but I mean it in all innocence. The girls of Vietnam are the most beautiful on earth, in my opinion— though I have just enough basic psychology to realize that I may believe it because my own mother was one of them. In any event, I think your path is clearly marked. It isn't Lord Buddha you need to encounter beside a placid pool, but a grave young lady trailing her fingers through the water."

"I already have encountered one," Belgard whispered.

"Yes? Where?"

Belgard indicated the Chinese game.

Tinh Hoa set the glass of water aside and picked up the game.

"Have you ever seen one of those before?" Belgard asked. The burst of emotion had drained him; he felt dull and misshapen.

"Yes."

"I don't know what it's called."

"It's called Xim Xam," said Tinh Hoa. "Rather—" he stopped.

"Rather what?"

"I was going to say, the uncorrupt version is called Xim Xam. . . . Do you consider me a broad-minded man, mon vieux?"

"Certainly."

"*This* offends me."

"Why?"

"Do you believe in God?"

"No."

"What do you believe in?"

"I'm not sure any more. Man."

"Then ignorance and degradation would offend you—"

"Yes."

"Xim Xam," said Tinh Hoa, "is a ritual performed primarily by the cu si—the laymen monks—in front of the altar of Quan Cong. The officiant makes a request of the deity and then shakes a container of sticks, something like this one. The first stick that falls out bears the deity's response. European gypsies do rather the same thing with cards. 'Will I marry the prince?' asks the young girl. 'You will,' says the gypsy, 'and you will bear five handsome children, travel a great distance, and receive an important message by mail.' The young girl's heart beats faster, the gypsy goes away a few francs richer, and no one is hurt. But suppose the gypsy were to say, 'No, you will never marry. You will be crushed by a train on the fourth of March, you will have both legs amputated, you will linger for three months in unspeakable agony, and when you die, it will be in silence and madness because your throat will no longer be able to muster a scream.'" Tinh Hoa paused. "Both responses are foolish—but one gives pleasure and one gives pain. I've seen cu si who fancied themselves sorcerers play the game you have on the table. They complicate it by falling into a trance—"

"They pass through a door."

"My friend," Tinh Hoa said, "there are fuses, and there are fuses."

"I have done it," Belgard muttered stubbornly.

"I see. And—what did you find on the other side?"

"The girl."

"Because you were lonely. If you'd been starving, you would have found food. What else was there?"

Belgard remembered the snap of the neck, the reddening of the water beneath the gray robe. "Nothing."

"Nothing at all?"

"Nothing important."

"You were fortunate. There are tales of cu si disappearing forever. I presume they were devoured by dragons. Which stick did you choose? Do you remember that?"

"The one by the glass."

"This?"

Belgard nodded, and Tinh Hoa turned the wand until he could see the ideograph at the end.

"The man who explained the game to me," Belgard went on, "said that the characters on the sticks were nouns—like 'garden.' As I understood it, the noun sets the theme, more or less, for what one would find on the other side of the door."

"Yes," Tinh Hoa replied slowly, "more or less. . . . Do you read Chinese, mon vieux?"

"No."

"May I ask a favor? Let me have the game. Let me burn it."

"You make the same mistake all censors make. You don't say, 'Stop it, it's dull,' you say, 'Stop it, it's exciting.' "

"Then at least break this stick and throw it away. Pick another. This character is 'shih.' " Light from the bedside lamp yellowed the ivory fingers as they twirled the stick around and around. " 'Shih,' " repeated Tinh Hoa, and looked up. " 'Corpse.' "

"What?"

"You've chosen 'corpse,' " Tinh Hoa said.

CHAPTER 12

IT WAS STILL DARK next morning when the orderlies came for him. The sleeping pill he'd been given had not quite worn off by the time the anesthetist added his preoperative tranquilizer, and Belgard wasn't trundled down the hall so much as he was sailed. His surroundings were fair, his companions witty, his fears illusory, his soul disembodied.

A number of jocose friends were gathered in the operating arena. He told them to belly up to the bar, the sodium pentathol was on him, which got a big laugh, and then he realized that none of them knew about Cookie, and this prompted him to begin a searching inquiry into the roots of American divorce. One of the nurses held his hand and told him she understood, but suggested that the answer wasn't to fight when someone lied to you, it was simply to lie back. Otherwise, she said, they'd have to strap him down.

"It hurts a great deal," he said.

"I know," Bobbie answered.

"They don't realize I'm not out," he said. "Don't let them start cutting—"

"It's over, Captain," Bobbie said. "You're back in your room."

"Listen," Belgard replied, "it was over a long time ago."

"Do you mean you expected it?"

"I think I must have."

"You could fly home, talk to her—"

"About what?"

"This isn't the newest problem in the world."

"Tell her that? Take her by the hand and remind her in a fatherly way that everyone makes mistakes? What mistakes? she'd ask. She loves Crying Freddie. She has thought about it for several days, and she has come to certain irrevocable conclusions. Crying Freddie needs her. Life will be an endless round of passion and tears and gaiety with Crying Freddie. It has not quite occurred to her yet that with a whole universe of single women running loose, Crying Freddie chose to screw a married one—but when it does, she won't believe that Crying Freddie was hedging his bet, she'll say that Fate led them to each other. She'll expect us all to get together from time to time—for Sunday dinner, for bridge—"

"No."

"Don't laugh. This is a strange woman."

"Captain—"

"I swear to you she'll expect me for Sunday dinner. She'll have a picture of herself humming in the kitchen while Crying Freddie and I have a cigar on the patio and discuss politics. She'll never believe that anything basic has changed. I wonder if she believes I'm a human being. She'll never grant me anger. That wouldn't be gallant on my part. Would it?"

"No."

"I feel better. How can that be?"

"You've had a good long sleep—"

"Bobbie?"

"No, Bobbie'll be back in the morning. I'm Grace."

"Hello, Grace."

"Hello, Captain."

"What time is it?"

"Almost dawn. Would you like another pill?'

"What have I been telling you?"

"Nothing important."

His eyes burned. It was hard to focus on anything past his own hand. The nurse's starched uniform was a white smudge in the darkness. Yet he could somehow see the door clearly defined behind her. The white uniform fluttered. The door began to open inward. "Grace!" he called sharply.

"Yes, Captain."

"Where are you going?"

"I'll be right back. Try to sleep."

"Don't go away!"

. . .

"Grace!"

. . .

He clambered off the cot and fled through the dank door to the barred window on the barracks side of the cell. The hot moonlight blinded him. The bars were razor-sharp; blood from his lacerated hands left black palm prints on the whitewashed wall. He pounded and howled, shouting Minh Chau's name over and over, until the guard on duty brought a relief guard on the double, a small cinnamon-haired M.P. who laid his scalp open for four bloody inches with one slash of his club and then guided him solicitously back to his bunk. "Goddamit, be careful," the first guard complained to the other. "This mother was an officer, they want him to look *nice* tomorrow, they gonna *invite* half the gook government, you want to pacify him, kick him in the goddam nuts or someplace, use your fuckin' head, man." "I'm sorry, Warren," the relief guard said. "Well, watch it," said Warren.

"What time is it?" Belgard gasped.

"You got more'n seven hours." Warren told him, "It ain't even ten yet. They ain't even got the fuckin' *scaffold* built yet."

"She's on her way," Belgard whispered. "She'll be there at ten." He struggled to sit up. "Oh, my God— my *God!*"

"Bugger won't learn, will he?" Warren said. "Chrissake, even a *dog'll* learn." He glanced around. "Where's our fag chaplain?"

"In the can," said the relief guard.

"*Again?*"

"He said it was too close in here. He said he had a ghastly headache."

"Bastard's probably got his period," said Warren. He brought his club down in a powerful arc across Belgard's crotch, and before Belgard fainted he heard him say "See?" to the relief guard and thought he heard the relief guard reply "Yeah" from the echoing icy distance, and then he was free of the cell, free of his body, off like Scrooge at Christmastime to witness more horror he could neither prevent, nor direct, nor cry out against, nor touch. . . .

CHAPTER 13

SAIGON HAS BEEN called the Paris of the East by generations of travelers who have never seen it. Its tamarind-lined streets are geometric and lack character. The squat stucco buildings were planned by French bureaucrats from Toulouse and Nantes, from Rheims and Bordeaux, and they no more resemble the shops of Paris than Djakarta's sewers resemble the canals of Amsterdam.

By nine-thirty, crowds had begun to gather near the Central Market, strolling along Le Loi Street or bicycling up the three miles of Tran Hung Dao Boulevard from Cholon. There was something medieval in the air, a promise of gore that no one could quite put his finger on, no one was quite certain of. Some said there would be a revolution; others, a beheading. But there were no speakers in the square, no block and ax, no banners.

Earlier it had rained; the older ladies in the audience avoided the puddles and scolded the bad boys who charged recklessly past and splashed mud on them. More than one parent complained that there was no respect left in the world and asserted bitterly that it had been far different in their day and that what was needed now was less permissiveness and more discipline. Girls floated past on high French heels, wearing pads beneath their ao dais to plump their thin Vietnamese buttocks out like Sophia Loren's. Here and there a Buddhist monk waited as patiently as a lizard on a rock, for something—some-one—for the show to begin.

It began at 10:03. Belgard, who was not there, saw it from a hundred simultaneous angles. An Edsel, which had proceeded like a stately barge up Vo di Nguy Street from the suburb of Khanh Hoi, on the other side of the Arroyo Chinois, halted at last before the shop of a Chinese tailor named Soong. Six persons—five monks in saffron and Tran Minh Chau, clad in a modest rust-colored robe—got out of the car. One of the monks offered Minh Chau two small white pills, which she chewed, and a pocket lighter; the others formed a semi-circle in the street. The crowd had sobered. Minh Chau's lovely face was pale and drawn; she leaned for support on the arm of the first monk.

Upon reaching the middle of the street, she paused to confer with the monk at her side. There seemed to be some problem about the pills. Several of the monks assured the girl in low caressing tones that the effect would be felt momentarily, and at length she allowed them to assist her to the pavement, where she assumed the lotus position and for some reason donned a pair of comically large sunglasses.

She kept her gaze on the street while two of the monks punctured a large tin and poured gasoline over her head and body. Apparently she had been expected to speak a few words during this act and had forgotten them, for the first monk, the eldest, motioned for the gasoline men to keep pouring while he leaned over and touched the girl on the cheek and murmured into her ear.

"What?" Minh Chau asked in French, and then said, in Vietnamese, "Yes, of course." She lifted her dripping face. "I follow Thich Tinh Hoa—" she began, but her voice faltered and the eldest monk was obliged to motion the gasoline pourers on and to whisper again to the girl.

The people on the fringes of the crowd had a difficult time hearing. "Tell her to speak up!" they shouted rudely. "What did she say? We can't hear a thing!"

"I follow—"

"Speak up! Speak up!"

"I follow Thich Tinh Hoa resolutely into Paradise!"

Then the pocket lighter wouldn't work. Minh Chau possessed beautiful fingernails—long, polished, and pointed—and she broke two of them on the stubborn lighter before she burst into tears and threw it away. Belgard heard her say, in French, "Oh, this is grotesque! I'm going home—"

But the eldest monk already had struck a kitchen match. As it spurted alive he said to the audience in ringing tones, "For Vietnam!" and then he touched the fire to Minh Chau's drenched hair.

The flames spread in a slippery blue wave from the girl's head to her shoulders, breast, and lap. At first she seemed too astounded to scream, as shocked as a swimmer who has stepped into a numbing lake. Then, when her skin began to blacken, she uttered a hoarse, terrible call, the word "God" in French—animalistic, masculine, mindless. A few persons started toward her, but the monks formed a pious ring to keep them back. While the girl rocked and shrieked, the monks sent appropriate prayers to Lord Buddha on her behalf and prudently drew their skirts away from the fire.

It took her an unconscionably long time to die. Even after the heat had seared her lungs, she managed certain throaty sounds now and then, which disturbed a few of the onlookers even more than the shrieks had. A newsboy—an Indian—saw that the Edsel's left-hand window was down, and he commenced to toot its horn to cover the noises. Others in the crowd rushed to imitate him, and soon the din was unbearable. The girl had toppled onto her side, leg bones fused into the lotus position, arms upraised to cradle the partially destroyed head. Cambric handkerchief to his nose, the eldest monk conducted a brief visual examination to determine whether or not Minh Chau was beyond help and then trudged away while his colleagues passed out ink-wet pamphlets denouncing Madame Nhu and the Diem regime.

In the distance, police sirens could be heard as the honking horns died away one by one. Hastily the monks piled back into the Edsel. There was a moment of undignified panic when the wheezing motor wouldn't start, but it chugged over at last, and with mournful faces the monks sped off in one direction while the police entered from another.

The charred object in the street had become stuck fast to the melted asphalt. No one seemed to know how best to remove it, and no one thought to cover it, so it continued to lie on view in its supplicatory position until morning, when an Army disaster squad took it away, asphalt and all.

CHAPTER 14

THE WHACK of hammers into wood reminded him that he had one small continuing problem of his own: he was to be hanged on a new scaffold before an invited important audience today.

He couldn't think how Bobbie had penetrated into the cell. He wanted to tell her about the bizarre mistreatment he'd suffered at the hands of the two guards—about the girlish disappearance of the chaplain whenever he was most required—but something held him back.

The underside of his tongue ached; his lips were clenched around a slippery glass straw. "O.K., let's see how we're doing here," Bobbie said. She pulled the straw out of his mouth and squinted at it and said, "Well, *good*," in a pleased way. She shook the thermometer briskly. "Don't look so troubled. It's right on the nose. How do you feel?"

At last Belgard whispered, "Like some crazy bastard cut my stomach open."

"Listen, that was no crazy bastard, that was an artist. You had some grade-A problems in there. I felt like applauding when he got through."

"How long have I been out?"

"It's four-thirty—off and on for about thirty-four hours."

The hammering recommenced; Bobbie followed his gaze to the open screened window.

"Does that bother you?" she asked. "Would you like me to close the window?"

"What's happening?"

"They're building a scaffold."

Belgard settled his eyes on hers.

"I'll close it," Bobbie said.

"Just a minute," Belgard said. "What kind of a scaffold? Why?"

"Well, as I understand it," Bobbie said, "they have these ceremonies every May eighth—"

"Buddha's birthday."

"Yes. They march up Thong Nhut, and they give some speeches in the Botanical Gardens and put on some little shows for the kids. Anyway, that's the puppet booth— Punch is hanged, you know, he goes to hell." She drew the curtains. "Maybe you can see it."

The low orange sun blinded him.

"Hey, there's your friend," Bobbie said.

"What friend?"

"There, coming in—the monk, Thich Whatever."

Memories danced and played just out of his mind's reach. "He's coming to see me," Belgard said.

"I imagine so."

"Don't let him."

"What?"

"This room faces west—"

There were ways to ward off the five demons, and the con hoa, the ma, the quy, the malevolent spirits. Rhinoceros horn would do it, or the axes called luoi cam set.

The octagonal talisman with the mirrored center would bar them even from a western-facing room.

"Really, that's fascinating," Bobbie said. "Where did you hear about—what? Thuong? You must have made a study of these things."

Someone rapped on the door.

"Lock it!" Belgard whispered, but it was far too late, far too late, he nearly understood the mystery now.

"Are you awake, mon vieux?" Thich Tinh Hoa would ask.

The shaven head appeared uncertainly around the opening door. "Are you awake, mon vieux?" asked Thich Tinh Hoa.

Time was a toy track, beginning where it ended, circular and repetitious—the same billboards, the same tunnels, the same rending accidents. He had been there before.

"Am I disturbing you? A friend called me from the airport—just in from Paris, like a new season, like spring. We were in the neighborhood; I thought of you, mon cher—"

No.

"Permit me to present Captain Jack Belgard. This is Tran Minh Chau."

She was wearing an elegant ao dai, high-collared, sheath-slim; a conical straw hat dangled by a blue chin ribbon from her slender left hand. Love and despair and horror left him speechless.

Doubtfully, the girl glanced at Thich Tinh Hoa. "Why is he so frightened?" she inquired in French.

Her perfume was Parisian; her slanted eyes were black, her finger tips red as blood.

Bobbie had poured him a glass of water. "Have a drink, Captain."

It was a situation that even Tinh Hoa seemed unable to cope with. "Shall we sit down?" He found a chair for the girl. "Sit here."

"I can't stay."

"You will," Belgard said in French.

"I can't."

"You'll be back."

The girl arched an eyebrow. "I really think not."

She drifted past Tinh Hoa, out of the room. "I'll wait for you in the car, Uncle."

Tinh Hoa stared at Belgard and then at Bobbie, and then left without another word.

The hammering had stopped; the scaffold was built. Several children had brought their pets for an airing in the park. Belgard could hear them laughing and calling beneath his window. Outside, a monkey with a thin silver chain around its neck ran to and fro like a madman.

CHAPTER 15

THE OPERATION was performed Friday morning. On Saturday, he was allowed to sit on the side of the bed, and by Sunday he could reach the lavatory unaided. When he was asked how he felt, he smiled and nodded amiably, and it really wasn't until the nurses and the therapists began to compare notes that they discovered he hadn't spoken a word since the girl and Tinh Hoa had left his room.

It was difficult to take the problem seriously at first. His temperature and blood pressure were normal; his appetite was good; his elimination regular. Everyone agreed that the incision was a model of its kind, and several of the younger doctors made repeated trips to view it.

But by Tuesday, Bobbie had grown concerned enough about him to report the situation to the staff psychiatrist. This man, Jackson, questioned her closely about Belgard's attitude prior to Tinh Hoa's visit and wanted to know if Belgard had discussed his wife's letter with her. Bobbie said he hadn't, which now struck her as strange. She said two more letters had come for him in the meantime—both from Glendale, California, but neither in his wife's hand—and though he'd opened them she had the peculiar feeling that he hadn't read them yet.

"Because he wasn't interested?" Jackson asked. "Or because he just didn't care to read them in front of you?"

"No, he didn't seem interested," Bobbie said.

Jackson sent for Belgard's records, studied them, and on Thursday, the ninth of May, made a point of dropping by Belgard's room. The captain wasn't there, but Jackson did surprise Bobbie furtively reading the first letter, the one from Cookie. Although she flushed scarlet, she insisted that it was due to rage rather than guilt. She told Jackson what the letter contained. She said that she had run across some evil bitches in her time, but never one quite so noisome as this.

"Where's the captain now?" Jackson asked.

"Outside."

"Has he started talking again yet?"

"Not a word."

Jackson proceeded thoughtfully toward the patio.

CHAPTER 16

ONE OF THE ORDERLIES had set up a lounge for Belgard under a lime tree near the eastern border of the Botanical Gardens. They were feeding the animals in the small zoo there, and the distant roars of the two captive lions had put the neighborhood's dogs' nerves on edge. Belgard was trying to identify a few of the breeds from the different bays and howls and yips when someone said, "Quite a racket, isn't it?"

A man in lightweight civilian trousers and shirt sleeves had stopped in the grass beside him. The man pointed off now with the stem of an unlighted pipe. "The dogs," he said.

"Oh," Belgard said. "Yes."

The stranger glanced down and then held out his hand. "My name's Jackson, by the way. I'm on the staff here."

"Belgard," Belgard said, and shook Jackson's hand.

"Mind if I join you?"

"Not at all. There's a chair"—Belgard craned his neck—"I think on the walk. Do you see it?"

Jackson fetched the chair. He placed it beside Belgard's

and collapsed into it, sighing. "Well—how do you feel?"

"Very fine."

"Anxious to return to duty?"

"Is anyone ever anxious for that?"

"Oh, some are—some aren't," Jackson said. "I talked to your surgeon. He said you'd been champing at the bit to get back—before the operation."

"Well—"

"I know. It's an odd war. It's hard to stay passionate over a stalemate. Especially when half the people at home don't give a damn anyway."

The roaring had stopped. The lions were being fed now.

"I'm a psychiatrist," Jackson continued. "Some of the people around here have been a little concerned about you."

Presently Belgard said, "Why?"

"Well," Jackson said, "if you were a doctor, wouldn't you be concerned over a patient who wouldn't talk? Wouldn't you presume he might need help?"

"I think I'd presume he wanted to be left alone," Belgard said.

"But if that were the case, he wouldn't have tried to draw attention to himself by not talking, would he?"

Belgard looked back at the livid low clouds that had begun to gather in the west.

"Captain?"

"No, I don't suppose he would," Belgard said.

"Some men scream when they're wounded; some just sit in the shell hole and wait."

"Why?"

"Oh, many reasons. The man who waits might be proud of his self-control. He might be afraid the enemy'd see him if he moved. He might even have seen someone he loved move—and get shot down because of it."

"Not my father, if you're getting Freudian," Belgard said. "I didn't have a father."

"Oh? What happened to him?"

"I don't know. He ran off with a neighbor's wife when I was four."

"Very dramatic."

"He was a damn fool. He thought he was Gauguin."

"Do you mean he ran off to Tahiti?"

"Almost. Mexico. He'd just been made president of his company. He kicked the whole thing down the drain. Job, home, family—we never saw him again."

"Is he dead?"

"I told you, I don't know; he's as good as dead, as far as I'm concerned."

"So—at four you became head of the family."

"Yes."

"Big responsibility."

"Only in my own mind."

"That's where it counts, Captain."

The sun kept appearing and disappearing behind the clouds. Belgard covered his eyes against the glare. "I can't see that this is getting us anywhere."

"Are you married?" Jackson asked.

"I am married," Belgard said. "My wife's getting a divorce."

"And—how do you feel about that?"

Puzzled, Belgard lowered his hand. "How do I *feel*?"

"Do you love her?"

"Well, certainly I love her. I *loved* her."

"Why 'certainly'?"

"What?"

"Describe her for me."

"Well, she's pretty—"

"Is she intelligent?"

"No. She's childlike. Naïve. Uninhibited."

"Did she love you?" Jackson asked.

"I think so."

"Then why are you divorcing?"

"She—ran off with another man," Belgard said.

"That doesn't sound as though she loved you very much."

"No, it doesn't."

"You'd never have done anything like that to her, would you, Captain."

"No."

"Why not?"

"I told you—I loved her."

"Which three things did you love about her most?"

Belgard stared at the lime branches above his head.

"Any three," Jackson said helpfully.

"Well, I can't think when you jump me like that."

"Her sense of humor?"

"No. She didn't have one. She depended on shock value. She'd tell a story, and she'd use the word 'fuck' in it, and everybody would laugh because the word would be coming out of such a pretty young face."

"Would you laugh?" Jackson asked.

Belgard looked at him and then gazed back at the branches. "No," he said.

"Was she sexually interesting to you?"

"She was very ticklish," Belgard said. "I used to try to caress her—and she'd giggle and shudder. I finally gave up trying."

"She'd shudder?"

There was no answer.

"What were you thinking then, Captain?" Jackson asked.

"I was thinking about a French film of Cocteau's," Belgard answered. " 'Beauty and the Beast.' I was trying to remember why Beauty stayed with an object she found so ugly and fearful."

"Gratitude, wasn't it?"

"Was it?"

"Do you think the analogy applies in your case?"

"No."

"Why not?"

Belgard rubbed his temple absently. "Because I don't think the Beast would have had such trouble finding three qualities to admire in his love. You've got me wondering now why *I* didn't leave *her*."

"And why didn't you?"

"I don't know."

"Is your mother alive?"

"No."

"How did she die?"

"She had a heart attack. I was twenty."

"Had she remarried?"

"No."

"How had you lived all those years?"

"My father left several thousand dollars behind—and then I started working as soon as I was old enough."

"You supported her, in other words."

"Not really; she always had a job."

"Do you mean she could have gotten along without your contribution?"

"Oh, yes—"

"But you stayed home and worked anyway?"

"Of course."

"Why 'of course'? Many men wouldn't have stayed."

"Again," Belgard said, "I just don't see the parallel here."

Jackson sucked at the stem of his dead pipe and then tapped the bowl on the sole of his shoe. "Well, maybe there isn't one," he said. "How did you feel, Captain, when your mother died? Can you remember?"

"Mad," Belgard said, "and relieved."

"And when your wife left?"

Belgard's feet had begun to cramp; he pressed heavily on the ground. "Look, this might be very interesting to go into," he said, "but I just don't have the time. She's already established residence in Nevada. She'd been there a week when I got the letter. I've wasted another week sitting around here. I only have a month left—"

"To do what?"

"Go *back* there! Talk to her. Reason with her."

"You've decided to fight the divorce?"

"Not—fight it—if that's what she wants. . . . To— tell her what a damn fool she's making of herself."

"Point out the dangers—"

"Yes."

"Save her from getting hurt—"

"All right."

"That's very noble."

"I can't help how it seems to you."

"It seems primarily like a lot of trouble to put yourself to for a woman you don't love. . . . You could write all this in a letter, couldn't you?"

"It wouldn't be the same."

"You have to appear in person—"

"I've gone over it and over it, and nothing else makes any sense! It's a matter of—"

"A matter of what?"

"Nothing."

"Life and death?"

Belgard clamped his teeth shut.

"Whose life or death?" Jackson persisted. "Yours? Do you have to return to America? Or do you have to leave Vietnam?"

"I'm not afraid."

"Nobody said you were."

"I'm not crazy, either."

"What about dreams?" Jackson asked. "Have you—"

"I don't dream!" Belgard shouted. His heart pounded; his hands gripping the arms of the wheel chair felt slippery and sore. He let his head fall back against the pillow behind him. "Jesus."

Soon he heard Jackson say, "Would you like to go inside, Captain?"

"No."

"Cigarette?"

"Maybe I *am* crazy."

"I don't think so."

It had grown darker. The sky pouched out, heavy with rain.

Belgard said, "I have always—all my life—believed in whatever I could see, hear, touch, smell, taste. That's basic. We start with that. I play with this other crap the way you play at any party game—the way kids scare themselves with horror movies—but, my God, my God, you don't *believe* it."

"What other crap?"

"Ghosts, mysticism, tea leaves—it's an excuse—"

"For what?"

"Fun, weakness—my dumb goddam *mother* believed in that."

"A game for children—"

"Absolutely."

"And you're a man."

Belgard watched the clouds boil closer. "I wonder."

"Why? What happened, Captain? Did you see a ghost?"

After a long moment, Belgard said, "Something like that. Not exactly."

"At any rate, something unreasonable occurred."

"Something unreasonable seemed to."

"Well," Jackson said, "it would shake up any scientist to see ectoplasm—wouldn't it."

Belgard pressed his fingers outward across his brow above the bridge of his nose. "All right," he said finally, "so the question becomes: *why* did he see it?"

"All right," Jackson repeated. "Why?"

The fingers massaged the brow.

Jackson waited.

"But that isn't the prime question, is it," Belgard said.

"Isn't it?"

Tired, Belgard said, "Quote: Who steals my purse steals trash—but he who filches from me my rationalization, I'd like to kick right in the crotch."

"Unquote," Jackson said.

Belgard filled his lungs to bursting, let the air out through pursed lips. "O.K.," he said. "Noble Jack Belgard doesn't give a filtered fart about saving Pitiful Misled Cookie, check?"

"Check."

"For such a little thing, she's been a heavy weight to drag."

"Weight doesn't depend on size," Jackson said. "Try measuring an albatross sometime."

"O.K., step number two," Belgard said. "If the captain doesn't want to rush home to save his wife from the Fate She Deserves, why *does* he want to rush home?"

"Answer?"

"To save himself. From ghoulies and ghosties and long-legged beasties—"

"And things that go bump in the night?"

"Unquote," said Belgard.

"We'd better go in," Jackson said. "It's going to rain in a minute."

"Now isn't that funny," said Belgard. "I've never seen it clearer."

"Clear enough to talk about what bumped you?"

"Imagination bumped me."

"What happened?"

"I had a dream—and the other day the first part of the dream came true."

"Precognition."

"What? Yes."

"Can you explain it?" Jackson asked.

"I think so."

"Go ahead."

"Well, I think there are two parts to it," Belgard said. "I had a dream—about a girl—"

"Yes."

"In which certain words were said—certain events took place—"

"Yes."

"All right, later on I met a girl who looked vaguely like the one in the dream. She was Vietnamese, so her hair was black, she was dressed in an ao dai, and so forth. After that, it was probably easy to fill in the other similarities—subconsciously."

"It's called 'bridging,' " Jackson said. "The mind wants to make chaos orderly. So it sometimes bridges the gap between what happened and what should have happened. It selects what it wants to see in the present, and it alters the part in the memory that no longer fits."

"Do you mean I created my own memory of that dream?"

"Is that harder to believe," Jackson asked, "than the phenomenon of precognition?"

"No. . . ."

"How long do you usually remember your dreams, Captain?"

"No more than a day."

"Do you remember any other dreams involving this girl?"

Belgard stared at the churning sky.

"Captain?"

"Yes, I do," Belgard said.

"Fine," Jackson said. "Here's a control we can work. Tell me everything you remember about it. Every last detail. Then if you ever think it's reoccurred, or that it's reoccurring, you can check with me."

Belgard hadn't realized that he'd filled his lungs again. He expelled his breath angrily, and then he began to laugh.

"What's the matter?" Jackson inquired.

"Doctor, you've got the patience of Job," Belgard said. "No. Forget the dream. Every indulgence is a step backward. No. I'm all right."

"Don't be too tough on yourself. Indulgence isn't such a terrible crime. You've been under some fancy pressures."

"I've manufactured some fancy pressures."

"Still—"

"No. The ectoplasm turned out to be cheesecloth. I can hear it, see it, touch it, smell it, taste it. The psyche was sprained a little, just sprained. We don't have to put a plaster cast around it. Let me exercise the thing, for Christ's sake, will you, please?"

Jackson's mouth smiled, though the eyes remained reflective. "Time to rise up and march with the rest of the army?"

"Right along there like a big boy."

The first drops of rain had begun to spatter against the leaves. Ambulatory patients were limping back to the hospital's side door; orderlies hurried toward the wheel chairs scattered across the lawn. Jackson brought his hands lightly down on his knees and got to his feet.

"O.K.?" Belgard asked.

"It's your sprain," Jackson said.

CHAPTER 17

IT WAS AS THOUGH he had come back finally from a repellent vacation, a trip through a wasteland of bad inns and meaningless landmarks. He'd had a terrible time. He didn't want to talk about it. He plunged into the business of catching up with the week he'd lost.

The two letters from California were fat with wrath and advice. It turned out that Cookie and her beau had not been as circumspect as prudence, or even common courtesy, required. Cookie had asked several girl friends for guidance after she'd discovered the immortal love she bore for Crying Freddie and had apparently alienated nearly all of them by going along with a disorganized hysteric whose current mate beat her black and blue nightly. This emotional cripple, whom Cookie had not been able to abide two months before, had become her most solemn favorite by counseling haste and other wise moves. "Isn't there something you can do, Jack?" the first letter ended. *"Isn't* there *something anybody* can do!!!"

The second letter was more considered and thoughtful. "Dear Jack," it began, "I'm sorry, but how many times did I tell you—*why the hell don't you kick that bitch's butt right up between her shoulder blades?*"

"I should have, you know," Belgard mused aloud. "I was remiss."

"Should have what?" Bobbie asked.

"Kicked that bitch's butt right up between her shoulder blades."

"Pretty long reach, isn't it, from here to Las Vegas?"

"So," Belgard said. "You've read these letters."

"Ah," Bobbie said. "*Well*. I'll tell you the truth. I do have this one tiny little flaw. I pry."

"Is that right."

"When I'm *motivated*."

"Motivated."

"I wanted to see where you'd gone. I missed you."

"It was a hectic trip. I don't recommend it."

"How do you feel about her now?"

"She should inherit a hotel with a hundred rooms," Belgard said, "and be found dead in every one of them."

"Very healthy attitude," Bobbie said. "You're coming along nicely."

"Nicely for what?"

"Hm?" Bobbie asked. "Oh—" She walked past him to the window, round-hipped and clean, smelling of soap. She flicked dust off the curtain in a pensive domestic way and then picked the morning's edition of the hospital newspaper off the table where the orderly had tossed it and handed it to Belgard. "Here, read your paper," she said. "I'll—" She headed back toward the door.

"Bobbie," Belgard said.

"What."

"You missed me?"

"Well, *missed*. I wouldn't say *missed*." She gave him a defiant, surprised look. "Boy, what a cocky assumption."

Belgard grinned. "Bobbie," he said, "what are you doing Tuesday?"

"Working."

"After work."

"I happen to have a thing on every Tuesday," Bobbie
said. "Listen, don't come along *too* nicely—"

"You know, it's like dancing," Belgard said. "You sit
out so long you think you've forgotten how—but you
don't."

"Listen—" Bobbie said again and broke off. She opened
the door. "Just read your paper."

"I'll see you Tuesday."

"You'll see me on *duty* Tuesday."

"Is the Calypso on Pasteur Street still open? Do you
like Vietnamese food? We'll have cha gio—"

"Why, they're not going to let you go wandering
around Saigon like some—"

"What time are you off duty?"

"Well, *six*, but—"

"You go home; I'll get a cab—"

"I *told* you I play bridge every Tuesday."

"Bridge? No—"

"Well, I *do*, every Tuesday. I can't—"

"How about eight o'clock," Belgard said, "or is that
too early?"

"No—"

"Fine. Give me your address and I'll pick you up at
eight."

"I meant no, I—" Abruptly Bobbie closed her mouth.
She began to laugh helplessly. "It *is* like dancing a little,
isn't it?" She fingered the short blonde hair that cupped
the back of her head; her vision already had turned inward, toward a closet, Belgard expected, filled with unsuitable rags, the anxious feminine hallucination of nothing

to wear, no time to shop in, no friends to appeal to. "They're not going to let you out, you know," she said. "You're supposed to stay put for two weeks."

"Create a diversion," Belgard said. "Start a fire in another wing. I'll flee during the resultant panic."

"Listen, I mean it," Bobbie said.

"Who'll be on the floor? Grace?"

"Grace—"

"Tell Grace to cooperate. Forget the bed check. We'll sneak back before the day shift shows up."

"If we're caught, it's going to be so long, Charlie," Bobbie warned him.

"We won't be caught."

"I must be crazy just standing here listening to you rant," Bobbie said. Confounded, she left the room.

Belgard got up and checked the window. The rain had warped the wood, but it moved in its frame, though noisily. There was less than a three-foot drop to a flower garden. He returned to the bed and opened his newspaper.

The lead story indicated that the Buddhist crisis precipitated by events at Hué on Wednesday was continuing to deepen. The death toll of Buddhists felled by government gunfire stood at nine. Scores had been injured, including the venerable Thich Tinh Hoa. Riots had broken out from Pleiku in the north to My Tho in the delta. Responsible voices were calling for a public apology by President Diem.

Belgard rose and looked out into the hall, but there was no one visible to call to. He sat down again in a chair by the door and went through the paper page by page, and gradually the outlines of the tragedy of May eighth began to emerge.

On the sixth of May, regulations against giving any religious flag precedence over the flag of the South Vietnamese nation had been reinvoked by Diem in Saigon. But the circular announcing the order had not reached Hué until Tuesday, the seventh. By then, the entire city was caught up in the precelebration of Lord Buddha's birthday; flags flapped and dangled from private poles as well as public buildings. Stung by the government actions, men and women converged on the Thu Duc pagoda for solace and explanations. Resentment against the Catholic president simmered all during the hot long night, and by morning antigovernment posters were everywhere.

Though Buddhist leaders strove to maintain discipline, rumors soon swept the crowd that even more repressive measures would be revealed that night at the Hué radio station, on the south bank of the River of Perfumes, and by eight o'clock the crush before the small stucco building had clogged traffic for miles.

Antiriot measures were invoked by Province Chief Nguyen Van Dang. Police were called to protect the station's property and employees; firemen used giant hoses to try to drive the mob off the veranda. At this point Assistant Province Chief Major Dang Sy arrived with several armored cars. And here eyewitness accounts became muddied. It was agreed that two explosions marked Major Dang Sy's entry into the packed courtyard. But Buddhists swore that they had come from the lead troop carrier; Dang Sy swore that they had not. Fearful that the explosions marked a Cong attack, the major drew his gun and fired three shots into the air, a prearranged signal authorizing his soldiers to use force if necessary to protect themselves. Fifteen American-supplied MK III concussion grenades were hurled. The crowd fled. Nine Vietnamese, including a child, were blown to bits.

Belgard's door squeaked open; Bobbie put her head in. "Captain?"

"Here," Belgard said.

Bobbie leaned farther around the door. "Oh. Are you awake?"

"What? Yes."

"A friend's outside to see you. He says he *could* come back at the regular visiting hours if you're tired or—"

"What friend?"

"A Sergeant Grainger?"

Surprised, Belgard folded the newspaper and braced his hands on the chair arms, ready to rise. "Howard?" he called.

"Yes, sir," Grainger said from the hall.

"Well, get on in here!" Belgard ordered.

Grainger's ears sprouted whitely below his brand-new haircut. The crease in his pants was sharp as a sword; his shoes gleamed. He grinned widely, as Belgard pumped his hand, and kept saying, "Now look out for the stitches, sit down, Captain, sit down, sit down—"

"Well, how the hell are you, Howard?"

"Just fine. Sir—"

"You're looking good."

"Try not to stay too long, Sergeant, O.K.?" Bobbie said. "Visitors aren't supposed to be allowed in until four, but we're putty in his hands."

"Yes, ma'am," Grainger said.

"Oh," Belgard said, "Bobbie—listen, could you do me a favor?"

"Sure."

"I want to find out if my Buddhist friend is all right."

"Why, what happened?"

"He was in Hué last Wednesday—"

"Oh, really? In the riot? My God, wasn't that terrible?" Bobbie included Grainger. "Did you read about that?"

"Yes, ma'am," Grainger said, "I tell you that was one

mother of a mess—" Blood poured into his white ears. "I mean—"

"Yeah, I know what you mean," Bobbie said.

"Call Doc Lap again, would you, Bobbie?" Belgard asked. "See if he's still up north, and if he is, where I can write to him. He may be in one of the hospitals up there."

"Gee, that's a shame," Bobbie said.

"Thich Tinh Hoa," Belgard reminded her.

"I remember," Bobbie said, and disappeared.

Still crimson with embarrassment, Grainger muttered, "She never understood what I meant, do you think?"

"Naw," Belgard assured him.

"I've been out in those bloody hills too long—"

"Don't worry about it."

"That's a pretty girl, Captain."

"Yes, she is."

"I think she likes you," Grainger said. "She about giggled herself to pieces when I asked if I could see you."

"Did she?" Belgard grinned.

"Shame to waste all that on a married man."

"Oh, I don't know," Belgard said.

Grainger cocked his eyebrows. "What's this?"

"We get along," Belgard said. "Something tells me we're going to get along better and better."

"Ah-*hah*," Grainger said. "Que sera, sera, right?"

"Right."

"I can see I'm gonna have to shoot a toe off or something," Grainger continued, "get myself a nice bed, nice giggly nurse—what do they have for the noncoms, gooks?"

"If you haven't tried it, don't knock it," Belgard said.

"God *Almighty*," Grainger said, "what have you been *up* to since you left us, Captain? No goddam wonder you look so—"

For a split second—for no longer than it took a shutter lid to blink across a fast lens—the rotted door stood ajar past Grainger's shoulder. Candlelight fell like a weightless yellow shawl over the bare shoulders of the girl on the low bed. His fingers found the swollen young breasts. One of Minh Chau's naked forearms covered her eyes. Her free hand guided him; her lips breathed, "Seigneur. . . ." He pressed his face into her black hair. "Sauvage—femme —Eve. . . ."

"I'm sorry," Belgard said. "What?"

"I say it's no wonder you look so pale."

"I'm a fraud," Belgard said. "I just talk a good game."

"You sure you haven't got one of them cute little brownskins hidden up your sleeve there, Captain?"

"Only in my dreams, Sergeant."

"Yeah, well, just don't throw that pipe away without givin' me a couple of drags. I been away from home as long as you have."

"I didn't use a pipe," Belgard said. "It was that bitch of a game."

Grainger chuckled, and then remembered the cylinder. "That—you mean the *Chinese* game? The one you found? You tried it?"

"I tried it," Belgard said.

"Well, how'd it work?"

"It didn't work at all. It gave me a couple of nightmares."

"Why? Where'd you go? Did you see the future?"

"Oh, come on."

"Huh?"

"Howard, the future's an accident. You have a billion choices, you make a billion decisions; it's not foreordained."

"The billion futures are, aren't they? Maybe you saw the one that—"

" 'Billion' was the wrong word. There are an infinity of choices."

"No," Grainger said.

"Sergeant, look—"

"No," Grainger said stubbornly. "Could you choose to be a horse tomorrow?"

"I suppose not."

"Then there may be billions of choices—but if you can't be a horse, you can't talk about infinity. Now, if you saw yourself as a horse, then you had a nightmare. But if you see yourself screwing a gook, why couldn't that be a part of your future?"

"That," Belgard conceded, laughing, "could be."

"So—"

"But the rest of the crap I dreamed couldn't, I can promise you."

"Why not?"

"I just couldn't go that route."

"Why?"

"Howard," Belgard said, "I have a certain number of free choices out of that billion."

"It looks that way."

"It *is* that way."

"All right," Grainger said, "suppose a space ship landed over at IBM, and these little green men came across this computer and pushed the button—wouldn't it look like the computer was making some free choices? If the computer had a soul, wouldn't *it* figure it was making some free choices? Particularly if one of its orders was to *believe* the choice was free every time the question came up?"

"We're all computers, are we?"

"I think we're all sure-as-hell programed," Grainger said. "I think experience does it, pain does it, I think our *parents* do it, *school*—and I think that narrows those billions of choices down some. Maybe what you saw was the only future possible—I mean, from the way you were programed to start with."

"So"—Belgard smiled—"every time I make what I think is a free choice, I'm really just locking myself a little straighter on target."

"Maybe."

"I don't know, I might as well kill myself now, then," Belgard said.

"Why?"

"Well, I'm going to end up dead anyway," Belgard replied. "I murder this friend of mine and they hang me."

Grainger watched him reflectively for a moment; then he lit a thin black cigar and sat back in his chair and crossed one calf over the other knee. "Oh, well, that's a bunch of horse shit," he said.

Belgard guffawed until tears came to his eyes.

Grainger grinned self-consciously. "Well, Captain, I thought you were talking about screwing *gooks*."

"You're a good man, Sergeant," Belgard said. "You're a breath of fresh air down these ether-filled corridors."

"Who is it you murder—anybody I know?"

"Why, have you got a candidate?"

"Well, sir," Grainger said, "I mean as long as it's in the unchangeable future, you might as well kill two dirty birds with the one stone, make a lot of deserving people happy."

"Who did you have in mind?"

"How about Major Finney?" Grainger suggested.

Belgard weighed his answers and then decided he'd heard a clumsy joke, nothing more. "Sorry, Sergeant," he said. "Officers are out of bounds. Pick again."

"Yes, sir."

"How's Dodd," Belgard asked, "speaking of officers?"

"Oh, he's fine," Grainger said, "fine."

"I really miss the camp. Did you get your rice planted?"

"Well—no," Grainger said.

Belgard studied the sunburned face. "What happened?"

"Captain," Grainger said uncomfortably, "back in the coal country where I come from they've got a saying: it's hard to talk about hell without mentioning the devil's name."

"So mention it," Belgard said.

"It's going to offend you—"

"I've been offended a lot lately," Belgard said. "I imagine I'll survive. We're in a hospital room. You're Howard Grainger, I'm Jack Belgard, no titles. Now go ahead."

"All right," Grainger said. He'd been brushing the nap of his cap; he hung it on his knee and sat back. "I think the major's won," he went on, "and I'm surprised at how mad it's made me, how wrong it seems."

"Won how?"

"The orders came through the day you left. Postpone the rice cultivation, postpone the small-arms training, prepare to pack up the records and move out."

"*Prepare* to move out."

"Yes."

"But you're still there."

"As of today, we're still there. I don't know how long it'll last."

"I feel," Belgard said finally, "like I've been on Mars for the last twenty years. Or off with the lotus-eaters. I am ready to vomit from all this lotus I've eaten. Have you ever felt like that?"

"Lotus?" Grainger said vaguely.

"I am glutted with lotus," Belgard said. "I am going to stick my finger down my throat, Sergeant, so stand back; I don't want to get any on you."

"Should I call the nurse?"

"What?" Belgard asked. Then: "No—no." His eye fell on the Hué story in the newspaper, on the mention of Thich Tinh Hoa. "Where's Finney now?"

"He's still in Saigon here," Grainger said. "As far as we know. At least he wasn't in Ton That this morning when I changed planes." He cleared his throat. "Dodd didn't want to bother you with all this business, but—I don't know—I had a couple of days coming. . . . I don't give a damn one way or the other about what happens to those bare-assed bastards, but—it's a good camp—we built a good camp—we're trying—*they're* trying—and then this pitiful misfit comes along—"

"Sergeant," Belgard began.

"Yes, Jack," Grainger said courteously, and waited.

"O.K., O.K.," Belgard said at last.

"Comes along and fucks it all up," Grainger finished. "What can we do? Anything?"

"I had two allies I was counting on," Belgard mused. "One's dead, one's hurt. I hate to call on General Harkins blind, but I don't see any other way now."

"When do you think you'd be able to get over there?"

"Not before Friday—"

"Not before Friday what?" the psychiatrist, Jackson, asked from the door. He waited politely, half in the room and half out, wagging the unlit pipe between his teeth.

"Oh, good morning, come on in," Belgard said.

Grainger had risen.

"Sergeant Grainger—Dr. Jackson."

"Sergeant—"

"How do you do, sir."

"Not before Friday what?" Jackson repeated to Belgard.

"Well," Belgard said, "we've got a timing problem.

There are a couple of things I have to do around town, a couple of people I have to see."

"In regard to—?"

"My current post. It's a matter of communication: I command a Montagnard training camp near Ton That—certain people want to disband it—"

"And you want it to continue."

"Yes."

"What does this have to do with your wife? Anything?"

"My—? No. Why?"

"I just wondered," Jackson said.

"No, nothing at all," Belgard said. "I don't think."

"Well, you seem to be in pretty good shape to me," Jackson said. "Your chart's O.K. I don't believe you have to be bound by that two-week stricture. You've been up every day, haven't you?"

"Every day."

"Tire easily?"

"No."

"All right," Jackson said, "you can peel out of here—oh, on Tuesday if you want."

"Doctor," Belgard said.

"Yes."

"You didn't happen to meet a wild-eyed nurse in the hall?"

"Well," Jackson replied. "Yeah."

"I thought you just might have."

"The thing to try to remember," Jackson said, "is that Woman is above all practical. If she has to jump in and out of windows, she'll jump—but it isn't the jumping, per se, that attracts her. She might tear her nylons. She'd rather drift down the front steps on your arm. This has the added advantage of making the other nurses jealous. So she asked me a simple practical question: Was it possible for you to get a pass on Tuesday? I considered the matter and said yes."

"You have my gratitude," Belgard said. "I wasn't too hot on that window ploy myself, to tell you the truth."

Jackson wagged the pipestem and started away. "Have a good time."

At the door, he met Bobbie coming back and executed a nimble little side step that she imitated automatically and very well, bumping directly into him.

"Have they ever thought of a revolving door for this room?" Jackson asked.

"No, I don't believe they have," Bobbie said mechanically. She looked pale and angry. "Excuse me."

"Is everything all right?"

"Oh, I'm a little mad," Bobbie said, "but it's O.K."

She smiled and stood aside for Jackson, who nodded back toward Grainger.

"Glad to have met you, Sergeant."

"Yes, sir, same here," Grainger said.

When the door had squeaked shut behind Jackson, Bobbie picked up an ash tray from the bedside table and slammed it down hard beside Grainger, who jumped and dropped his ash on the floor. "Oh—sorry," Grainger said.

"Don't *worry* about it," Bobbie said.

"Bobbie," Belgard began in a thoughtful tone.

"Oh," Bobbie said. "I got hold of one of those mumble-mouths at the Doc Lap?"

"Yes, good—"

"And I asked him about your friend, and he said he *had* been in the hospital, but he was out now. He said he was with his family in Can Dop Cau. Does that make sense?"

"Can Dop Cau's in the delta, isn't it?" Belgard asked Grainger.

"Yeah, down there past Tan An," Grainger said. "Pretty little place."

"Well, listen," Belgard said, "did they say he was all right? Can he have visitors?"

"Yes, he's fine," Bobbie said.

"This man's my best bet, Howard. He's a monk. He's a personal friend of Colonel Tai's—"

"Kind of go in the back door there," Grainger said.

"That's it. I'll get a jeep Wednesday—"

"Why wait?" Bobbie said. "You're cleared to leave on Tuesday. Didn't Jackson mention that?"

"Yes, ma'am, he did," Belgard said. "But I've got a date on Tuesday."

"Not with me, you haven't." Bobbie laughed. "Unless you can hitch a ride to Korea." Her nostrils were white and pinched. "Boy, I just hope I meet that tramp down some dark alley one of these nights," she added and laughed again.

"What tramp?" Belgard asked blankly.

"We have a captain of nurses here," Bobbie said, "who—" She broke off. "Well, never mind. We don't get along. We never have. She's been trying to get me transferred for months. She finally made it. I heard I'm due in Seoul on Monday morning."

"Well," Belgard said, "can't you—?" and stopped. "Well, for Christ's sake," he said.

"We could run away and desert," Bobbie said.

"Yes," Belgard said.

"Boy," Bobbie sighed. Eyes closed, she rubbed the back of her head, her neck.

"What if you spoke to this fellow who was just in here," Grainger suggested to Belgard.

"No, it's all set," Bobbie said. "She said she told me two weeks ago, but she didn't. She said if I was going to whine around I should have done it then. Damned smelly old fool."

"I'll talk to Jackson anyway," Belgard said.

"Listen, will you write?" Bobbie asked.

"I'll get you back here, don't worry," Belgard said. "Or I'll get to Seoul on my next leave."

"You say it, but you won't do it," Bobbie said. "I saw the look in that floozy's eye. She'll flutter those dumb false eyelashes and that'll be it. A bird in the hand's worth two in the bush, no matter what color the bird is. I also hate men."

"Now what are you talking about?" Belgard asked.

"Men."

"What floozy?"

"That floozy who was here with Thich Whatever. The niece."

"Minh Chau? I'm never going to see that girl again," Belgard said.

"It's her great-grandfather your friend's staying with in Can Dop Cau. She's there, too. If you go down there, *you'll* see her."

"No!"

"What's the matter, are you afraid?"

"No. . . ."

"It's Fate," Bobbie said. "You can't fight the old fickle finger."

Belgard looked at Grainger. Grainger's eyes were unblinking on his.

"Sergeant," Belgard said, "that isn't a computer I hear clicking, is it?"

"No, sir," Grainger replied. "That's superstition."

Belgard grinned.

But there was a chill in the air all the same, and miles away, down the distant circular track, something rocked and shrieked and called on God and burned to death.

CHAPTER 18

THE VILLAGE of Can Dop Cau, in the northern Mekong delta, was composed of five hamlets, which seemed to the geomancers to fall roughly into the shape of a bridge, a cau, though the emperor who had assigned it its name had simply picked the word out of the blue. This impressive coincidence had not only got the village off to a strong mystic start but had sustained it through floods and droughts and wars that would have swamped an average settlement. If a man from Can Dop Cau were to lose a leg in an accident, the gossips would shrug and say, "Well, there you are, anyone else would have died of gangrene, they're just lucky, those people."

Partly because of its sunny reputation, and partly because it lay like a ¢ sign across the national road that connected Saigon to the south, its population by 1963 had swollen to more than four thousand souls, all of whom had decided to stand in the highway and pick their noses at Belgard's approach. ("Honk," Belgard kept snapping to the young corporal who was driving him. "Keep your hand on the horn and keep moving; you're not going to kill anybody." "Yessir," muttered the corporal tensely.)

—130—

In addition to the pedestrians, there was the rain and the mud. From the time they'd left the hospital, the morning had been marred by one squall after another, and Belgard was soaked through in spite of the fact that the jeep was covered. He'd given up trying to find a comfortable position for his leg; he felt a brother's compassion for the outraged chickens in their sour crates on back of the motor scooters and on top of the buses. Finally, to frost the cake, there were the roadblocks—six in the first thirty miles out of Cholon, another on the outskirts of the first of the five hamlets. The Cong, Belgard and his driver were warned, had had an active week end. It would be wiser to return to Saigon. Two civilians had been killed in My Thuan; the UNESCO-sponsored School of Fundamental Education in Khanh Tho had been burned to the ground. Once a French-speaking South Vietnamese officer confessed to Belgard in a bone-tired voice that he had no faith left in the newly launched Ap Chien Luoc, the Strategic Hamlet Program. He said that the self-defense guards could keep the raiders out during the day, but that they were continuing to slip through the barbed wire at night. He said his own father had been slain in a fortified village only the week before. "I ought to be home," he said, "protecting my family." His eyes had the absent look of a man who already had deserted in all the important ways. Only his body remained behind.

"Now lessee, sir," said the young corporal, "uh—where do you think we ought to—uh—"

"What?" Belgard said. "Oh." They were inching past a thatched food shop; a middle-aged Chinese stood in the doorway, eating a thick sandwich of fried bread and pork fat. "Hold it," Belgard said. The corporal hit his brakes. Belgard leaned into the drumming rain. "Excuse me!" he shouted. "Do you speak French, mon vieux?"

"But yes, certainly," answered the Chinese in an effeminate Alsace accent.

"We search for the Buddhist pagoda! Can you aid us?"

"Go straight ahead to the first footpath. Turn left. You will see a building with a tile roof near an ancient gnarled tree. There you will have arrived."

"This is far?"

"No, no, straight ahead."

"Thank you, mon vieux!"

"It's nothing."

Belgard drew his head in and mopped his face on a rough wet towel. "Straight on to the first footpath."

The muscles in his lame leg twitched and pulled; he had a gloomy presentiment that he would bear all this discomfort, come all this way, only to find at the end that Tinh Hoa had left ten minutes earlier for Saigon.

"Oops," said the corporal and flattened the brake pedal again. The jeep skidded majestically across the road and sank hub deep into a rain-pocked paddy. The corporal ran his hands up and down the rim of the steering wheel before he glanced at Belgard. "I believe we just passed the first footpath, Captain."

"*Did* we."

"You stay here, sir. I'll—"

He dove into the downpour. Belgard listened to the corporal splash and flail down the road and then splash and flail his way back. With terrible patience, Belgard turned his head when the younger man bobbed up at his window.

"Sir—"

"Yes, Corporal."

"I don't believe I know what I'm doing out here."

"Ah," Belgard said. "Well, I'm glad to hear you say that. It makes me feel less alone in my own confusion."

The corporal wiped the end of his nose and pursed his lips and watched Belgard.

"Corporal," Belgard said, "will you kindly get this goddam vehicle back on the track?"

"Yes, *sir*," said the corporal. He floundered forward, threw up the hood, and glared at the drenched wiring.

Belgard examined his clasped fingers and then got out of the jeep and slogged head down through the mire back to the footpath.

The shower had increased to a deluge by the time he gained the shelter of the pagoda porch. The structure was wooden, old and plain; the door was open, but he could see no one in the main room. He knocked, and called in French, "Hello, is anyone there?" but the wind tore the words out of his mouth as soon as he had uttered them, and no one heard—or at least no one responded—and after a decent interval he entered.

CHAPTER 19

THE SANCTUARY smelled of boiled rice and wet reed mats. There were a number of altars in the room; a figure of Buddha dominated the far end, squinting down in gilded astonishment at the eighteen arms of the goddess Chu An De Phat Mau as she crouched at his feet. The other statues, except for the dreadful Chinese warrior Quan Cong, were unfamiliar to Belgard.

He was examining the polychrome face of a husky wood chopper seated on a tree stump when a voice at his elbow said in French, "He called himself Ong Dam."

A round, shaven-headed woman, little taller than a dwarf, stood beside him in the shadows. A rust-colored robe enveloped her from throat to heels.

"I'm the Superior of this nunnery," she explained in a whisper that barely carried over the machine-gun pop of the rain on the wooden roof. "You're in a Buddhist temple. Perhaps you didn't know."

"Yes, I knew," Belgard replied. "I was looking for a friend of mine. The Venerable Tinh Hoa."

"He was quite unlettered, but in spite of that he would chant all day long, 'I adore the Buddha A Di Da,' " said the Reverend Superior. She rubbed a wrinkled finger across Ong Dam's peaceful face. "And so in time he was proclaimed Bo Tat—a saint—the lowest order, true, but a saint, you see, nonetheless." She placed her free hand on Belgard's forearm; palsy transmitted itself to him like a feeble electric shock. "Let Ong Dam be an example to all of us," she whispered. "Adore, adore."

Someone approached behind a flickering candle. "Who is it?" The accent was Parisian, familiar.

"Good afternoon, Mademoiselle," Belgard said. "How nice to see you again."

The storm had released the girl's soft straight hair once and for all from the wavy discipline of the beauty shop. She resembled a doomed little spy in her beige raincoat. She was uncertain about Belgard's identity. "Yes?" she said. "I'm—sorry—"

"Captain Belgard," Belgard said. "The rude American in the hospital?"

"Ah." The lovely eyes grew noncommittal. "Surely. How does it go, Captain." She wasn't interested in an answer; she didn't wait for one. "I suppose you've come to see my uncle for some reason."

"Yes."

"He isn't here."

"In Can Dop Cau?"

"No, here—in the pagoda." She closed her mouth. The conversation was over so far as she was concerned.

"Well," said Belgard, "could you direct me to his home, then."

"I'm quite hungry," the Reverend Superior informed Minh Chau in a tone of patience and surprise.

"Your soup is ready, Ba Than," the girl replied in Vietnamese.

"Oh dear, soup?"

"Good clear soup."

"I cannot abide soup," the Reverend Superior complained to Belgard, "especially that watery kind."

"I don't blame you a bit," Belgard answered, "but it'll probably warm your stomach."

"Will it, do you think?"

"I do."

The Reverend Superior gave a grumpy sigh and padded off into the darkness.

Minh Chau was gazing contemplatively at Belgard when he glanced around. "You speak Vietnamese," she said at last.

"A little."

"More than any other American I've ever met. More than most Frenchmen."

"You called her 'Ba Than,'" Belgard said. "Was that out of respect, or—"

"No. She's really my mother."

"I see."

"She became a nun after my father was killed. The Directress of the Buddhist Studies Association allows her to stay on here because of my uncle primarily. She's harmless—but her mind tends to wander a little. There are three other nuns to take care of the temple. Ba Than only comes by on ritual days."

Belgard thought. "Fourteenth of May? What's that?"

"Sam Hoi. Buddha's forgiveness is asked on the fourteenth and thirtieth of every month."

"Are you a Buddhist?"

"I'm not sure. I think I may be. It's far easier for me to know what I'm not."

"Easier to be anti something than pro."

"Yes."

"Like—anti-American?"

Minh Chau's gaze met his again. "Yes, like that. It's nothing personal."

"I'm glad to hear it."

"I'm not going to be drawn into an argument about politics, Captain—"

"I didn't mean to start one."

"But can you give me one sensible reason why any government would choose to support that monster in the Gia Long Palace?"

"He's the elected leader of this country."

"He's a narrow-minded bigot. He's out to suppress Buddhism any way he can. What do you call that insane act of May eighth?"

"I understood the ban was on all nongovernment flags: Catholic, Buddhist, Cao Dai—"

"The ban was proclaimed forty-eight hours before Buddha's birthday, when the flags were already up. It didn't occur forty-eight hours before a Catholic holiday, did it?"

"President Diem isn't a man notorious for his tact, Mademoiselle. I can certainly imagine him banning Catholic posters on Christmas. He wants to instill a sense of Vietnamese nationalism in the—"

"But he *didn't* ban anything on Christmas. Did he?"

"No."

"And he *did* create a crisis in Hué. And there *was* a riot. And nine people *were* slaughtered. My uncle had a grandstand seat to those particular murders. You really ought to talk to him about it. It might open your eyes."

"It might—if they're indeed closed."

"There's one thing I truly admire in the Americans," Minh Chau said. "They're so certain of everything. Never a doubt. Not a—" The percussive plosion of the French word "pas" snuffed out her candle.

Solemn as a censor, Belgard located his Zippo, struck it.

At last the girl thrust the dead wick into the flame. "I expect," she said in a tone of choked fury, "that you're the type who believes that all women—especially young women—should remain entirely uncommitted: toys to play with, never a thought in their pretty curly heads—"

"Not at all," Belgard said.

"Well, there's no longer room in this attic for toys. I consider myself as committed to my country's fight for honor and survival as any warrior in the field. I loathe Vietnam's enemies as deeply—"

"Diem? The Americans?"

"Diem, the Americans, the Communists—and probably, if you want the fact, in that order! Vietnam's a strong man in a shallow stream, it seems to me, drowning from an excess of rescuers. They have *got* to be thrown off!"

"I'm not sure the stream is that shallow, Mademoiselle —or the rescuers that evil."

"You wouldn't be. How long have you been in my country, Captain?"

"Forgive me," Belgard replied. "But how long have *you* been in it?"

Stung, Minh Chau cried, "I didn't ask to be shipped to France as a child! I was born here, at least! I came back as soon as I had a choice! I *know* where I belong! Attending classes in Paris doesn't make one a French school-girl, Captain!"

"Nor does passion necessarily make one a crusader. Wars aren't won by suicide brigades—"

"No one said anything about suicide."

Belgard stopped short. "No. They didn't."

"It seems a remarkably pointless argument to bring up."

"I was thinking," Belgard said, "of the grand gesture, the baseless martyrdom—"

"Yes," Minh Chau said with a sharp humorless laugh, "well, you don't have to be concerned about *me* and martyrdom. I happen to believe in life. I'd never waver on that score."

"Good."

"Unless there were simply nothing else to look forward to."

"There's always something else."

"You're quite wrong. Suppose God were to die, for instance."

"One creates one's own gods, Mademoiselle. In case of death, one ought just to create a replacement."

"If you really believe that, then we're even more different from each other than I'd presumed."

"Mademoiselle," Belgard said, "you mentioned that you might be a Buddhist. Didn't Buddha preach *dis*passion?"

"Perhaps I'm not a Buddhist," replied Minh Chau. "More and more I think I'm not. More and more I think I may be a Tinh Hoaist."

"Mademoiselle!"

The cool young gaze played over the fat shape of a merry Buddha across whose plump stomach six little figures frolicked. "It shocks you?"

"Your uncle," Belgard went on, "is a man. Not a god."

"Gods give one courage; gods are wise, strong; so is he."

"Gods—"

"Captain," Minh Chau interrupted, "I haven't asked you to agree with me. You raised a point and I disputed it. If I happen to feel that something is irreplaceable, isn't that my business?"

"Certainly," Belgard said.

"You don't intend to destroy him just to prove I'm wrong, I hope."

"No."

"Then let's agree to disagree and let it go at that. All right?" She cocked her head, listening. "Well, the rain's stopped anyhow." She blew out the candle and put it on the main altar and buttoned her raincoat around her throat. "Come along, I'll show you where the house is."

She stopped at the pagoda door. Belgard hadn't moved. "Captain?"

At length Belgard turned. "You know," he said, "I think perhaps I'd better go on back. I find I still feel a little shaky."

Minh Chau shrugged. "Whatever you like. I'll tell him you were here. I know he's planning to return to the Doc Lap in a few days. You were probably fated to have your meeting there all along." She gave Belgard a crooked smile. "And one can't fight Fate, after all."

Belgard straightened. "Well, we discover another source of disagreement," he said.

"Oh?" said Minh Chau. "Fate's like God, then—one creates one's own?"

"Exactly," Belgard said. Joining her, he took her elbow. "Let's find the house, Mademoiselle, before the rain recommences—shall we?"

CHAPTER 20

HEAT LAY LIKE laundry steam over the five hamlets, piercing to the lungs, almost visible. They trudged back along the footpath to the road, where the corporal, apparently turned to stone, still hung motionlessly over the clogged black bowels of the jeep. The girl pointed out the roof of the house to Belgard, and Belgard cranked the corporal up and around until the corporal said that he saw it, too. He assured Belgard that he would have everything running in apple-pie order before you could say Jack Robinson, and he promised to pick Belgard up in fifteen minutes.

Two particolored goats and a dog that smelled of age and rain came to greet Minh Chau when she appeared at the wrought-iron gate. The old dog barked crossly at Belgard and one of the goats tried to butt him. "It's all right, I'm not a Diem-ite," Belgard told them in Vietnamese; Minh Chau's mask of granite disapproval cracked, though by the time they'd reached the rococo veranda she had managed to mend the damage. "I'll see if my uncle's awake," she said.

"I'm very impressed with this house," Belgard said. He pointed. "Is that a fish pool?"

"Yes."

He ran his hand over one of the fluted columns that supported the veranda. "Beautiful."

Holding the bright green front door half open, Minh Chau said, "What you really seem is terribly surprised. What did you expect? A thatched hut?"

"Nothing this elegant."

"I find it pretentious."

"Indeed? Why?"

"It's neither fish nor fowl. Thatch at least would be honest."

"Honest? Or Vietnamese?"

"The two are the same."

"Not at all," Belgard said. "Thatch is a matter of economics, not beauty—not nationalism."

"Can we agree on anything whatsoever, do you think?" Minh Chau snapped. "What day of the week is this?"

"Tuesday."

"There! I knew we'd stumble onto some sort of common ground if only we searched long enough. It *is* Tuesday."

"Not in my country," said Belgard.

Minh Chau's jaws dropped. "Captain—"

But it was too much for Belgard to sustain, and when he started to grin the girl's choked outrage turned into vexed low laughter. Thunder growled in the west.

"Oh, come in," she muttered, "before Thien Loi takes us both off."

"Who?"

"Can't you hear him?"

"Oh, the thunder."

Minh Chau nodded. "The Spirit of Heaven sends him down, to punish criminals—and probably men who tease women. He carries a bronze ax—"

"Very powerful talisman."

Minh Chau directed a puzzled look toward Belgard. "Yes. How did you know?"

"About luoi cam set? Well, you told me, didn't you?"

"No—"

Again the thunder reverberated over the flat plain. "I haven't thought about luoi cam set since I was a little girl," Minh Chau said. "I would have given anything for one then. . . . I actually had some powdered rhinoceros horn—"

"To ward off the five demons?"

"Yes—well, especially to keep Ba Hoa away. It's disappeared by now, though—the powdered horn."

"I'm not sure," Belgard said, "who Ba Hoa is."

"Ba Hoa?" Minh Chau smiled. "Oh, a terrible spirit. The Fire Goddess. Ba Hoa burns people to death." She held the green door graciously for him. "Captain?"

CHAPTER 21

THE MAIN ROOM was spacious and cool; palm fronds attached to the ceiling beams rustled overhead, and brightly colored paper streamers drifted through the dark air like seaweed. A pallid young man was sitting on the bench before the main ancestral altar. He rose when Minh Chau and Belgard entered, but Minh Chau ignored him. The cackle and chatter of numerous old women flowed from the kitchen area.

"This way, Captain," said Minh Chau.

Since he found himself passing directly in front of the wan young man, Belgard felt constrained to wish him a good afternoon in Vietnamese.

Startled, the young man returned the greeting and asked if he couldn't fetch Belgard a cup of water or a slice of pork or something.

"Oh, do sit down, Tan, please," Minh Chau said irritably, and the young man obeyed her at once. To Belgard, Minh Chau explained that she liked the *idea* of lam re, but that Van Tan had been underfoot for five days now and she was frankly ready to scream. "He's a nice boy," she confided to Belgard in French, "but my God, he's so dull. I just hope my poor cousin knows what she's doing."

"What," Belgard started to ask, "is lam re?" but the girl already had disappeared into a bedroom and was calling after him to follow, so he contented himself with shrugging sympathetically at the young man, who shrugged back and rested his elbows on his knees and placed his head in his hands.

In the bedroom, the girl was trimming a golden lamp on a squat teakwood table. "My dear, dear friend," Belgard heard Tinh Hoa say in a tired voice, "how kind of you to pay me this visit. You honor my house. But should you be traveling so soon after your surgery?"

Satisfied at last with the lamp, Minh Chau moved away from the bed into the shadows and Belgard was able to see Tinh Hoa for the first time. The beaten face was puffed to twice its size. The purple skin seemed about to split over the brows and cheekbones. Belgard stared, appalled. "Hoa!"

"Isn't he handsome?" Minh Chau asked. "Diem's masseurs know how to put a man in shape, don't they, Captain?"

Tinh Hoa was lying on top of the bed mat in an old-fashioned ankle-length European nightgown. Belgard clasped the thin hand held out to him. "But this is dreadful," he said in French. "I had no idea—"

"Oh, it was quite a performance," Tinh Hoa answered in the same language.

"You were at the radio station?"

"On the veranda. Trying, really like a fool, to disperse the crowd."

"He was lucky, to tell you the truth," Minh Chau said. "If the government police hadn't just beaten him to the ground, he would have had his head blown off."

"Yes, four of the men standing across from me were killed. It was frightful, like the Christian Hell—noise and fire and total disbelief in what was going on under one's nose—flesh raining down—blood as thick as fog—in-credible—" The whispery voice trailed off; the hand rest-ing in Belgard's trembled like a child's.

"Well, it's war now," said the girl. "Even the Ameri-cans won't be able to save Diem after this."

"I don't like to hear you use the word 'war,' " said Tinh Hoa. "We're waging peace."

"Cut his throat or love him to death," growled the girl, "it's all the same to me." She turned on her heel and left the room abruptly.

There was a rough wooden bench under the room's one window. Belgard pulled it to the bed, straddled it.

"She isn't as military as she sounds," Tinh Hoa said at last. "I hope you realize this isn't Jeanne d'Arc so much as Jeanne Moreau."

"I think you underestimate her sense of outrage," Bel-gard replied.

"Not at all. I know she's absolutely sincere. But I know as well that she's in search of stability rather than justice. She believes a good deal more at this point in me than in Vietnam."

"Do you know why?"

"Because I'm as safe as I am exciting. Because I seem to have found the far land she's looking for. I'm a country-man of hers, Captain, a kind of mulatto of the spirit, neither French nor Vietnamese—a Parisien rooted in Asia."

"This far land," Belgard said. "Is it Buddhism?"

"It is for me."

"And for the girl?"

"I don't know. Later, perhaps. When most of that great healthy passion of hers is spent. When all the bawl-ing children have popped out from between those strong young legs and gone swaggering off on their own."

"I think you love her, Tinh Hoa."

"No question of it."

"Then," Belgard said, "under the circumstances—in view of the tensions—wouldn't it be wiser to send her back to Paris as soon as possible?"

"I've suggested it," Tinh Hoa said. "She'd intended to until the day we visited you in the hospital."

"Why? I don't understand."

"She finds you attractive," said Tinh Hoa. "She's been badly spoiled by European men. Your arrogance took her off guard. If she's spoken once she's spoken a thousand times of your incivility. All the other men she's met have become her slaves. You ignored her. So of course you're the one she remembers."

"But, Tinh Hoa—"

"I'm sick of answering questions about you, mon vieux. If this was a campaign, it's been a masterful one. You ought to give lessons in how to disturb vain young girls."

Belgard closed his mouth and shook his head a little in disbelief. "It wasn't a campaign."

"Captain, don't look so downcast." Tinh Hoa smiled. "She'll recover, I assure you. Although you haven't helped things by turning up in Can Dop Cau. But then perhaps it wouldn't have mattered. As a devout Buddhist, I'm sure one has a lifetime of appointments to keep—Samarra after Samarra—struggle against them though we will. Don't you agree?"

"Absolutely not," Belgard said.

"Ah, be careful, Captain," Tinh Hoa said, laughing. "You'll confess to me next that you did have it plotted out, that you've meant all along for her to fall in love with you—to break her heart—to bring her to some dire Oriental end, while you strolled back to your ship like Lieutenant What's-His-Name."

"Pinkerton."

"Like Lieutenant Pinkerton. Not true?"

"Not true."

"Yet here you are, uncivil as ever. If you were worried about my health, couldn't you have written? It's a question that cries out for the severest self-examination, Captain—"

"I was worried over something more than your health, Venerable."

"I'm beginning to believe it."

"The Americans are planning to abandon the Ton That training camp."

While Belgard looked on, the monk's face began to grow visibly older, grayer. "I think," said Tinh Hoa, "you must be mistaken—"

"No. It's a fact." Belgard told Tinh Hoa what Sergeant Grainger had reported; how the rice planting had been postponed, about the preparations to move out.

"Then—how do they expect the Montagnards to defend themselves? They'll go over to the Cong; they'll have to! Ho's bound to send troops in! The way'll be wide open to Pleiku—"

"You haven't heard from Colonel Tai about this?"

"Not a word." Tinh Hoa looked around blindly. "What a time for it! The country divided, Catholic against Buddhist—Tai may not even be there by now. Diem may have removed him." He bent forward like a tumbler, almost double, to press his forehead against his knee. "Let me think."

"If Tai," Belgard began, "could talk to General Harkins—"

"No, I have it," Tinh Hoa said. He lifted his haggard face. "I'm sorry. I interrupted you."

"Go ahead."

"Well, it seems to me," Tinh Hoa went on, "that if I went to Diem myself—I was a schoolmate of his brother's, you know, I was on tu-toi terms with the whole family—if I went to him myself and drew his personal attention to the problem, asked him *personally* to intervene with Harkins—" He thrust his spindly legs over the side of the bed. "I'll return to Saigon this afternoon."

"Venerable—"

"There's no other way, Captain," Tinh Hoa said. "I tell you frankly that dealing with Diem, for me, is like nuzzling a whore, but if Vietnamese soldiers can die in the defense of their country, then I can certainly endure an hour's nausea."

"Will he cooperate with us, Venerable?"

"He will, once he's made aware of the crisis. He can't afford to lose the Montagnards to the Cong. He has vision enough left for that, at least. It may be faster for him to contact the American ambassador. We'll see. . . ."

"I don't know how to thank you for this, Venerable—"

"Mon cher, please. . . . Would you like to ride back with me?"

"I have a hospital jeep."

"Oh, you're still officially there? At the hospital? I mean, will you have to report in tonight?"

"No, no, I'm on my own until Friday. I'll have another examination then, and after that I'll be given some sort of extended convalescent leave. I'd like to try to get to Seoul."

"In Heaven's name, why?"

"A woman. My nurse. She was transferred there."

"The blonde?"

"Yes."

"Very attractive. You took my advice, then."

"Your—?"

"To seek an agreeable companion."

"Oh! That's right."

"Now, didn't you find flesh warmer than fantasy? I remember your intrigue with some creature in the Xim Xam box—"

"Much warmer," Belgard said.

"May I be frank? I was a little worried about you, Captain, that day."

"I was a little worried about myself," Belgard replied.

Tinh Hoa regarded him in silence for a moment and then clapped him briefly on the shoulder. "Well, to return to our sheep—I'll telephone you as soon as I've spoken to Diem. I'll demand an audience the moment I arrive. He may grant me one tonight. If he can't, or won't, I'll consult his chief of staff, another schoolmate—"

"Shall I try to contact Harkins at the same time?"

"Would it be practical? Are you acquainted with him? Would he recognize your name?"

"No."

"Then I wonder," Tinh Hoa said, "if it wouldn't be smarter, diplomatically speaking, to have this petition come specifically from the Vietnamese government—as a matter of national concern, you understand, rather than —forgive me—"

"Personal self-interest?" Belgard finished for him.

"Of course, if you'd rather—"

"No," Belgard said slowly. "No, let's go along with your instinct, Tinh Hoa."

"All right, I'll ring you at the hospital, then, as soon—"

He broke off at the rustle of silk outside the curtained doorway. "Uncle?" Minh Chau inquired.

"Come in, my dear."

She had removed the raincoat; she was wearing a French suit, shorter than the American styles Belgard remembered. "Tan's left," she said. "And the captain's driver is here."

"Tan?" the monk said in dismay. "Are you sure? Perhaps he's still in the kitchen."

"No—"

Tinh Hoa, who had started toward the door, stopped helplessly.

Bewildered, the girl asked, "But—what does it matter? You'll see him tomorrow."

"That's the trouble, I won't." He threw her a reproachful look. "I wish you'd called me."

"Well, but—"

"Oh, you couldn't have known."

"*Why* won't you see him?"

"I'll be in Saigon." He strode to the door and poked his head through the curtain. "Draw me a bath, someone!" he shouted in Vietamese.

"Is he serious?" Minh Chau asked Belgard, aghast. "What about the wedding?"

"Whose wedding?" Belgard began, but the girl already had left his side.

"Did you hear me?" Tinh Hoa was bellowing into the main room.

"Venerable," an old female voice bellowed back, "they could hear you in Imperial China! Yes, we heard you! It's being done!"

" 'Hear you in Imperial China!' " Tinh Hoa mocked in a furious mutter. "Damned old harridan." He stalked out of the room.

"Mademoiselle?" Belgard asked again. "Whose wedding?"

Minh Chau stood in the curtained doorway, biting one of her long fingernails. "What?"

"Whose—"

"My cousin's. Listen. You don't think you could persuade him to stay, do you?"

"Well—"

"It's enormously important."

"So is his reason for leaving."

"Politics?"

"Some friends of mine," Belgard said, "are in very, very grave danger. I think Thich Tinh Hoa may be the only one who can save them now."

"Americans?"

"No—Moi."

"Friends of yours, I thought you said."

"I did."

"*Moi?*"

In a few words Belgard told the girl about the camp, about the differences of opinion regarding its strategic importance, and about his and Tinh Hoa's concern for it. Minh Chau listened without interruption. "So," Belgard ended, "it may seem a small part of the whole picture, but—"

"Please, I understand," Minh Chau answered. She gnawed at the fingernail. "Of course, you're absolutely right. The camp is the important thing, not the wedding." Her eyes found Belgard's. "I'm amazed, you know—"

"About what?"

"Your success with the Montagnards. My father always felt that one of Diem's great weaknesses was his inability to bring the Moi once and for all onto the government's side. He said it wasn't enough to dismiss them as savages and expect them to remain ignorant and uncommitted. He said the Communists wouldn't make that mistake."

"I agree."

"But now you're doing Diem's work *for* him."

"It sounds to me as though your father would have done the same."

"Yes," said the girl.

"Your father was in politics, Mademoiselle?"

Minh Chau shook her head; her glance fell on Belgard's military insignia. "He was in the army. One of Diem's generals. He was assassinated by the Communists in nineteen fifty-nine."

"I'm sorry—"

"So were we all. He was a good man, an honest man— in many ways, I think, a naïve man. He believed in doing one's best—in trying. The odds were generally immaterial to him." She paused. "It's peculiar. He was short and rather plump, but I could never look at him without thinking of Don Quixote."

"I know the type," Belgard said.

Again the girl's eyes rested momentarily on him. "Yes," she said. At length she pushed through the curtained doorway. "Well, your driver's waiting, Captain," she said over her shoulder.

In the main hall, a number of candles had been lighted against the gloom. Two husky servant girls in calico blouses and black pantaloons were sweatily polishing the light-colored hardwood tables under the jaundiced eye of a tiny old man wearing a wispy gray goatee, the sign of wisdom. He acknowledged Minh Chau's bow with a distant nod and scolded the servant girls for leaving streaks on the French armoire and the loud pendulum clock.

"Ong Ke Hien," Minh explained in a low whisper. "My father's grandfather, the highest venerable in the cult committee. Very strict, very insistent on the old ways. I sometimes wonder how anyone in Can Dop Cau is ever going to get married properly once he dies. He's the only one left who remembers the true ritual. Of course he says that no one cares anyway. He maintains that the youngsters like my uncle have no respect for tradition nowadays, that all they're interested in is ease and wise-cracking and shortcuts."

"Sounds familiar."

"Doesn't it."

"This lam re you mentioned—"

"Well, there's a perfect example," said Minh Chau. "It means, literally, 'to be the son-in-law.' In the old days, a young man was expected to spend a certain amount of time serving his fiancée's family—principally in the fields, you know—to demonstrate his skill as a farmer and to prove that he was diligent and strong enough to support the girl of his choice. Now—" Her eyes twinkled. "Well, you saw what it's degenerated to. Boys like Van Tan turn up every day for a week before the wedding in their very best clothes, combed and brushed to within an inch of their lives, and drive everyone crazy getting in the way for half an hour or so."

"And how much longer will this go on?"

"On Van Tan's part? Oh, his lam re has ended. The wedding's tomorrow."

A pot shattered in the kitchen; voices climbed in denunciation of someone called Miss Big Bottom, the clumsiest servant girl, Belgard was given to understand, who ever had driven a bride's patient mother to the verge of madness.

"Both families help with the cooking," said Minh Chau, "although the reception will be at the groom's house. Van Tan and his father will come by tomorrow to bring my cousin her bridal costume and to inform her ancestors that the wedding is about to take place. Then everyone will troop back to Tan's home for the main ceremonies."

"And the feast."

"Yes, and the feast."

"It must be a happy occasion."

"Happy—beautiful—moving. At least that's the way I remember it. I haven't seen a Vietnamese wedding since I was a child." Smiling, Minh Chau twisted a loose golden bracelet around her wrist. "A young aunt of mine married a poet from Da Lat. I remember her red silk gown and her round hat and her grave eyes. All the children tried to make her laugh, because that would have been a marvelous scandal. The bride is supposed to be terribly solemn and this particular aunt was a dreadful giggler. But Ong Ke Hien had put the fear of Hell into her, and my aunt got through the entire ceremony without so much as a little snort. Then of course the dam broke, and at the very worst time. The bride, as it happens, is required to walk her parents to the edge of the farmstead after the ritual, to bid them good-by, and then to return reluctantly to her new husband, hiding her face as she quietly weeps. Well, the strain had been too much. My poor aunt forgot and started to skip—literally to skip like a schoolgirl—back to her handsome poet. Ong Ke Hien shouted at her, but it was too late. She stopped short—and then she began to laugh, and she laughed until she cried. So did all the rest of us—even the poet—even Ong Ke Hien. There never was a more wonderful wedding, I'm sure." Minh Chau grinned at someone past Belgard's shoulder. "Was there, mon cher?"

"Never," said Thich Tinh Hoa.

Belgard looked around.

"They're reheating my water," Tinh Hoa explained. "Miss Big Bottom tipped over the tub. Can you imagine?"

"Yes, I can," Minh Chau said.

"Captain," Tinh Hoa said, "it occurs to me that I've been a remarkably rude host. Since you don't have to be back at the hospital tonight, why in the world don't you stay here? There's plenty of room. Then you can see one of these celebrations for yourself tomorrow. I promise you'll never forget it."

"Oh—"

Tinh Hoa glanced at the girl for confirmation. "What do you think, niece? Wouldn't he enjoy that?"

Startled, Minh Chau said, "Well, certainly, if—"

"I'm sorry," said Belgard. "It's very kind of you, Venerable—Mademoiselle—but I have other plans."

"Break them," said Tinh Hoa.

"I'm sorry—"

"We insist. It's all settled. We absolutely won't take no for an answer."

"Uncle, dear," said Minh Chau through clenched teeth. "You're embarrassing the man. He has other *plans*."

"Really? Captain? Have you?" Tinh Hoa let his eyes rest for a speculative second on Minh Chau's angry scarlet face before directing them back to Belgard. "You're *certain* this isn't a campaign, mon vieux?"

Stiffly Belgard said, "Tinh Hoa—"

"All right, all right." Laughing, Tinh Hoa linked his arm through Belgard's and strolled with him across the room under the palm fronds and the rippling paper streamers to the front door. "But if you should change your mind, please don't hesitate to come back, do you promise? You'd be most, most welcome."

"Thank you."

"And try not to worry about your camp. I'm convinced the situation is far from lost."

At the door Belgard turned to bid the girl good-by, but she had vanished.

"Oh, I expect she's in the kitchen," Tinh Hoa. "I'll tell her you've gone."

"I feel very awkward about this," Belgard said. "I wish you hadn't teased her."

"But that's what nieces are for—to tease."

"Nevertheless—"

Tinh Hoa's regard grew contemplative. "You know, the interesting part, I think, isn't that I teased her, Captain —but that you object."

"What?"

"I'm beginning to wonder just who may be under siege in this particular war."

"My friend, don't be ridiculous," Belgard snapped. "What do you mean? Do you think I'm in love with her?"

"Strange word to choose," Tinh Hoa murmured. " 'Ridiculous.' "

"Well, it's laughable."

"Why?"

"*Well*—"

"Leo Tolstoy told once of a very exclusive club he longed to join as a child. But he was never able to pass the initiation. The first rule required one to stand in a corner and not think of a white bear for five minutes."

"Listen, Venerable—"

"Ever since you met this girl, Captain, you've looked to me like a man in a corner, do you know that?"

"In any case, why should my problems bother *you*?"

"Because it isn't a white bear you're dealing with!" Tinh Hoa exploded. "It's a human being. And when you torment *this* human being, you torment—" He broke off sharply. He stared for a moment at the knob in his hand, and then he passed his other hand over his shaven scalp. "Well," he muttered. "Isn't that interesting. Speaking of wars."

"Tinh Hoa—" Belgard began in an undertone.

"No, you're right," Tinh Hoa said. "It's none of my

business, none. It's strange, isn't it, how even the best of friends can find themselves at each other's throats for no reason at all. A philosopher might draw some profound parallels from that. East and West, Vietnam and America—" He stopped, held his hand out. "Truce, Captain? Shall we bow to the tiresome fact that allies need limitless patience with each other?"

Belgard let his breath out by degrees. When he could trust his voice, he said, "Let's do that, Venerable."

"Actually, it's myself I'm thinking of," Tinh Hoa said. "I looked at your face just then, and I thought, Now maybe you'd better ease your way outside, little monk, where you'll have some running room, and then I decided, no, make a quick thoughtless move like that and he's apt to forget himself and pitch you off the veranda and break your neck, and then the Army will have to hang *him*, and your poor niece will kill herself out of sheer melodramatic spite at the two of us, and then the Buddhists will blame the Americans, the Catholics will blame the Buddhists, the Chinese will blame everybody and invade, the President will drop the Bomb, and World War III will start—all because two friends with the best intentions in the world forgot themselves for one split second and moved too quickly." He drew the door open and held his hand out in the western style, smiling. "So have a good trip, mon vieux. I'll talk to you tomorrow at the latest."

The rain shivered like a plastic curtain between the edge of the veranda and the courtyard. Belgard's driver waited under the overhang; the jeep was nowhere to be seen. "Venerable, thank you again," Belgard said. "If there's ever any way at all I can return the favor—"

"Please."

"Good-by, good luck—"

"Equally, mon vieux."

Belgard hurried to the corporal's side. "All right, Corporal," he shouted, "let's swim for it! Where are we?"

He was halfway up the path to the gate before the corporal caught him. "Uh, sir!" the corporal shouted. Rain bounced crazily off his desperate face. His mouth worked, but the sounds were indistinct.

Belgard leaned closer. "What?"

"—doornail!" the corporal shouted.

Belgard contemplated him through the beaded downpour. Tinh Hoa had retreated into the house. They were alone in a sea of Vietnamese mud.

"I'm sorry, sir!"

"Are you saying," Belgard got out, "that you have failed to put that vehicle back in shape?"

"Sir, I'm not a mechanic!"

"But, if—"

"Sir, I can't *do* it! I've tightened everything that was loose and I've loosened everything that was tight and I've dried everything that was wet and the bastard won't *go!*" It was difficult to say for certain in the dancing rain, but it looked as though the man had begun to weep. "I'm an accountant! I didn't even know how to drive until they assigned me to the motor pool! Jesus Christ Almighty, what's the reason for this foolishness? Do you know who's in charge of Payroll out here? A spy." The corporal gave a wild laugh. "I swear on my mother's grave! I talked to him—they sent him to school for eight months to learn the secret *writing*, how to stuff the secret capsule up the *ass*, how to talk four languages, and there he sits, screwing up everybody's allotment because the one thing they *never* taught him was how to work the computer."

"All right, corporal," Belgard said.

"Sir, what are we gonna do?"

"About the car or life?"

"Either one. Sir."

"We're going to face the fact of them, stop giving them a meaning they can't possibly have, stop playing games, running like headless chickens. We are going to try to advance ourselves to the point of having the sense to come in out of the goddam rain!"

There was no bell on the bright green door, no knocker of any sort, so Belgard pounded on it with the side of his fist until it was opened a fearful crack by one of the servant girls. Her eyes held the absolute expectation of death. She was the youngest, the sacrifice. Two other girls crouched behind her, poised to flee.

"May I—" Belgard began in Vietnamese.

"No!" screamed the girl and slammed the door in his face. But on the very heels of the scream, before Belgard could close his surprised mouth, a slap resounded like a gunshot in the main room of the house—wails rose—feet ran—and the door was reopened at once. "Oh," said Minh Chau in a cool, indifferent tone, "it's you, Captain." Over her shoulder, she added, "It's all right, Uncle. It's only your friend."

Tinh Hoa's startled face appeared behind her. "Captain? Is something wrong?"

"You won't believe this, Venerable," Belgard began.

"Your car won't work."

"My car won't work," Belgard said.

"Come *in.*"

"I wonder," Belgard continued, "if you'd mind letting my driver ride back to Saigon with you."

"But not at *all.*"

"Then he can tell the hospital where I am, and they can send another car for me tomorrow."

Minh Chau raised her eyebrows slightly. "Tomorrow."

"After the wedding. Provided your gracious invitation is still open."

"My dear friend," said Tinh Hoa, "I can't tell you how happy this makes me. Us. How deeply honored. Of course it's still open. You're welcome to stay for a night —a week—the whole war."

"He'll have to take your room, you know," Minh Chau said.

"Yes, why not? It's the best room in the house." Mockingly Tinh Hoa added, "Unless you're afraid to face west, Captain, without so much as a thuong luong to protect you—that's a little eight-sided box with a mirror in the middle, to bar the five terrible Vietnamese demons. Half the village considers me a madman for not having one. The other half thinks I probably have something even more valuable buried under the floor. Like the Thunder God's ax, luoi cam set—extremely powerful talisman."

"He knows, Uncle," Minh Chau said. "You told him about luoi cam set before."

"No. Did I? When?"

"Here," Belgard said. "On a gray late afternoon like this. In the rain. . . ."

"No, surely not. You've never *been* here before—have you, mon cher?"

The toy train plodded around the circular track.

"I could swear I have," Belgard said.

"Oh, yes—I know the sensation," Tinh Hoa agreed.

"It seems to me," Belgard went on, "that the explanation we finally came up with, Venerable, was that I must have read about the talisman somewhere."

"Well, perhaps that's exactly what happened," Tinh Hoa said. "You read about it somewhere."

"Perhaps," Belgard whispered, "I did."

CHAPTER 22

By half past six, the changeable Vietnamese sky was clear again above the five hamlets. Though they were already half an hour late for the groom's party, Ong Ke Hien insisted that everyone march outside to wave good-by to Tinh Hoa and the corporal as the monk's 1950 Citroen went popping and gagging past the gate toward the National Highway. The women lined the drive like mutinous troops, cheering in a theatrical sullen way until the Citroen was out of sight, and then they plunged angrily back into the house to repair the wreckage to hair and costume as best they could.

Accompanied by the odorous old dog, who evidently had accepted his anti-Diem statements at face value, Belgard limped up the private road to the first bend and then leaned on the fence and smoked a cigarette and watched the air darken over the plain to the west. The ache in his leg was as much a part of him now as deafness to a gunner; he scarcely noticed it. The paddies, he saw, were almost empty. Most of the farmers had surrendered their fields to the night and the Cong at the first sign of sunset. He wondered if the Citroen should have set out quite so late. . . .

"Don't jump," Minh Chau said.

Jumping, Belgard whipped his head around.

Exasperated, Minh Chau said, "Well, I'm *sorry*, you know, but really what does one do about that? I coughed." She had not yet changed out of the short French suit. She wore small flared boots and carried the raincoat over one arm. "What if I'd tried to pass without a word and you'd seen me out of the corner of your eye? Wouldn't that have been worse?"

"Much worse."

"Ong Ke Hien and the others have left. I was sent to round up the strays."

"To—?"

"Roy Rogers and Gene Autry were very popular with the young girls in my lycée." In phonetic English, Minh Chau sang, " 'I'm back in the saddle again—' " She broke off, laughing. "My God, that absurd language of yours," she went on in French. "How does one ever learn it?"

"By fits and starts," Belgard said. "On tiptoe and in agony."

"Well, anyway—these groom parties are awfully casual affairs. You don't have to attend if you don't want to."

"I'd be delighted."

"My uncle left an extra razor in your room. There'll be hot water when you get back."

"Where are you going?"

"The pagoda. Ba Than's the other stray."

Belgard glanced at the starless sky. "Well—should you be walking around alone after dark?"

"How do you mean?"

"Maybe I'd better go with you. We were stopped at

half a dozen roadblocks on the way down. The Cong had a busy week end."

"Not here."

"Then they may be about due. Think what a prize you'd make. Tinh Hoa's niece. He'd pay almost any ransome to get you back."

"And—that's what you're really thinking of, the Venerable's pocketbook?"

"Naturally. What else?"

"I appreciate your logic, Captain," said the girl. "I accept your protection."

Her hand sought his in the dark; her fingers allowed themselves to be folded in his with such tender acquiescence, such unquestioning compliance, that Belgard stopped dead.

He could see the girl's pale face turn up to his. "What's the matter?" Minh Chau asked. "Why are you laughing?"

"Laughing?" Belgard said. "Was I?"

"God in Heaven," muttered the girl. "Here I am, in a savage land in the dead of night, surrounded by bloodthirsty hordes of Communist kidnapers, holding on for dear life to a lunatic."

"Do you know how old I feel right now?" Belgard asked. "About fourteen." He lifted their clasped hands. "It's this."

"What?"

"Touching you."

"Captain," Minh Chau said, "either that's the most sophisticated line I've ever heard—" She paused.

They continued for a moment along the road without speaking.

"No," Minh Chau resumed, "I'm not going to pretend that I don't understand what you mean, because of course I do." Her fingers moved against his. "You feel fourteen.

I feel as though I have very long hair, almost down to the middle of my back—and there's a new ribbon in it."

To the south, a pair of mortars had commenced coughing in a patriarchal way. They meant no harm to anyone, these mortars; they apologized for the flesh they shredded. A muscle in Minh Chau's wrist flinched at each contrite explosion.

"Are you frightened?" Belgard asked.

"No," Minh Chau said. "Yes. Not as much as if I had no one beside me, but a little."

Their road bent southward along the paddy's edge; they stopped to watch the reddish pulse on the horizon. The four-and-a-half-foot-high barbed-wire fence that surrounded the entire hamlet was sagging and rusty here; it swayed dangerously when Belgard prodded one of its rotted posts. A shallow ditch full of rain water lay just beyond. "They were supposed to dig that ditch twice as deep," Minh Chau said, "and fix sharpened bamboo stakes along the bottom, but you see what happened."

"Do the Cong ever come to Can Dop Cau?"

"Oh, yes—whenever they like. The fence has been cut in half a dozen places. No one has ever bothered to repair it, so they always return through the same holes."

"And no one bothers to wait there? To counterattack?"

"Is that what you'd do?"

"Yes."

"But then," said the girl, "you aren't Asian. You're the one who believes in fighting against the mandate of Heaven—in creating compliant new gods when the old ones become testy. You're a warrior. The villagers are fatalists. Most of them have a feeling that the war's already been decided."

"Your uncle's a villager—an Asian—and yet he agrees with me."

"Now that's the danger of short acquaintance. I don't think of him as Asian at all."

Belgard glanced at her and then nodded. "You're right," he amended. "I take it back. He's Vietnamese—but he isn't Asian."

"Neither was my father, oddly enough," said Minh Chau.

"He would have waited at the holes?"

"Yes," Minh Chau replied. "He would have waited." After a moment's reconsideration, she added, "Or he would have sent informers out to *hint* that he was waiting —so that he could have fallen on the raiders by surprise while they were cutting new holes somewhere else." The puffs of red lengthened along the belly of the sky; sound waves tapped more heavily against their eardrums. "What I'm trying to say," Minh Chau continued in a dogged, preoccupied cadence, "is that he was inventive as well as optimistic. He never seemed to lose the conviction that he was going to win. He knew exactly where he belonged, where his responsibilities lay. He was never afraid." Her hand had balled itself into a fist inside his. "Do you think that's possible?"

"Never to be afraid? No."

"*I'm* afraid."

"So am I."

She flicked her eyes toward the horizon. "Of that?"

"No—"

"What then?"

Belgard shook his head silently.

"Losing the conviction," Minh Chau whispered, "that you're going to win?"

Belgard raised her face with his free hand and slowly kissed her eyelids and then her mouth. Her body against his was as tractable as water conforming to the land. The sudden undammed experience of love dazed him. It wasn't a recurrence of love, it was his first inkling of it. He filled his lungs with her. His blood absorbed her like a drunk's.

"My God, my God," he heard her whisper. "Now what will I do if anything ever happens to you?"

Shaken, Belgard muttered, "Nothing's going to happen to either one of us."

"Never?" Her lips smiled sadly against his cheek. "We're in a fort we can't defend, mon cher. We simply can't get out of this life alive."

"Don Quixote wouldn't have agreed."

"Don Quixote had the advantage of us. He was mad."

"He was optimistic. I wonder sometimes if that isn't the ultimate sanity."

"How un-Buddhistic you are."

"Why?"

"To be angered by the idea of extinction rather than soothed by it. You want to fight instead of accept. Some things *are* foreordained, you know."

"I don't know it at this instant," Belgard said, "when I finally feel sane."

"Whom have you met who's lived forever, mon cher?"

"Whom have you met who hasn't been secretly convinced that he may be the first?"

Minh Chau's eyes searched his. Then: "Take the challenge? Fight whether we can win or not? Just because it's the optimistic thing?"

"The sane thing."

"All right." She pressed her face against his shoulder and repeated fiercely, "All *right*, I believe it, too. This war can be won. It'll end, and we'll have each other, and nothing will happen to you."

"Nor you," Belgard whispered, and held her head in the hollow of his two hands and kissed her warm mouth. "Nor you—"

CHAPTER 23

THEY RETRACED their steps without a word, allowing the old dog to herd them back to the dark veranda like a servant who expected his authority to be contested at every turn. The dog, who had been struck by a cart the year before and who really had not been the same dog since, hated the world outside the courtyard and dreaded accompanying any of the family past his own gate. He did it because he had to do it—because he always had done it—but the toll it took was severe. He generally suffered for hours afterward from nerves and a sluggish bladder, and he had nightmares when he slept.

"Look at him," Minh Chau said. "He knows he ought to go round up the rest of us—or at least make the attempt—but they've left a lamp on so that he can pretend we're all home."

The dog sniffed at the band of light that fell through the drawn curtains at the front window, then feigned surprised satisfaction and plodded away to his mat and his bad dreams.

Minh Chau opened the front door.

The altar had been hung with new silk; candlelight

splintered against the polished brass accouterments. The liquid sounds of a gamelan orchestra drifted from the back of the house.

"Thi Hai, my cousin," Minh Chau said. "Ordinarily, with Ong Ke Hien away, she'd be playing Elvis Presley records, but I expect she felt that sort of music wasn't innocent enough for the night before a wedding."

"She wasn't allowed to attend the party?"

"She mustn't see her new lord until he brings the red wedding gown tomorrow. Then they'll stand here—by the altar—while Ong Ke Hien holds a burning red candle and recites the ritual prayers. If the candle goes out, it's *very* bad. It means they'll have an unhappy marriage."

"Does the candle often go out?"

"The candle never goes out." Minh Chau grinned. "Ong Ke Hien drenches the wick in lighter fluid."

"Very prudent."

"Yes."

"What does the color red signify?"

Minh Chau mulled it over. "I'm not sure. The groom's robe is blue. . . . Yang and Yin perhaps. Red and blue— earth and heaven—body and soul. The colors have always seemed more satisfying to me, though, than white and black. Black's the color of confusion, white's the color of death, the absence of color."

"And blue?"

"Majesty."

"Red?"

"Hope. Sunrise. Birth. How western priests ever came to equate it with wickedness, I can't imagine."

"Probably they equated it first with excitement."

"And excitement is wicked?"

"To a man egotistical enough to set himself up as a confidant of God, anything uncontrollable would be wicked, wouldn't it?" The Balinese gamelan record had ended; now another took its place.

"Have you ever been to Bali?" Minh Chau asked dreamily.

"No."

"Indians call it the Morning of the World. We used to vacation at a very small hotel on the beach out of Den Pasar—one-story, eight or ten rooms; if it had a manager, no one ever saw him—at least I didn't. . . . I'd get up before dawn, while my mother and father were still asleep, and I'd run down to the sea, and I'd wade out in the shallow water until I was halfway between the reef and the land, and I'd watch the sky turn redder and redder—all alone there—while this immense thing happened. . . ."

She turned and whispered the word "Anh" when Belgard picked her up. She was as light as a Balinese dancer in Belgard's arms. Someone had lighted a red candle in Thich Tinh Hoa's room; the shadows trembled on the ceiling; the wedding music still penetrated the thin door.

"No red gown," Minh Chau whispered.

"Do you mind?"

"No. . . ."

Belgard kissed the lax long legs, the soft belly, the mystic sexual crease. "Nothing lovelier has ever lived than you, nothing—" Candlelight fell like a weightless yellow shawl across her shoulders. His fingers found the swollen young breasts. One of Minh Chau's naked forearms covered her eyes. Her free hand guided him; her lips breathed, "Lord. . . ." He pressed his face into her black hair. "Savage—wife—Eve. . . ."

"This is what red signifies—"

"Yes. . . ."

"This is the color of creation—"

"Yes. . . ."

CHAPTER 24

WHEN BA THAN, next morning, was informed that she had missed the groom's party, she was both astounded and inconsolable. She was very partial to the traditional snacks of betel leaves and areca nuts that were served at these affairs to symbolize unity and faithfulness, and though the women were sternly restricted to soft drinks by Ong Ke Hien, she would generally contrive to sneak a sip or two of rice wine over the course of the evening. She thought of it as medicinal; she believed it kept her calm during the dances and hullaballoo.

Ong Ke Hien, of course, demanded an explanation from Minh Chau the moment she appeared next morning. Deeply hurt, Minh Chau said that she couldn't understand what he was referring to. She said that she and Captain Belgard had covered half the village searching for the old woman, who, it seemed now, had been asleep the whole time in one of the nunnery cells. The fact was that she and Captain Belgard also had missed the party— or perhaps no one had *noticed* that. Then she started to cry. The bride-to-be burst into tears at this point as well, accusing Ong Ke Hien of dictatorship and a number of other sins, including gluttony.

"*Glut*tony!" Ong Ke Hien exclaimed. "*Glut*tony?"

"Oh, yes, you can't imagine what I'm talking about, can you!" Thi Hai screamed. "Well, that's perfectly agreeable to me, sir! Let's pretend it was never said! Never said, never discovered!" She threw herself into Ba Than's arms, sobbing as if her heart would break. Ba Than stroked her lovely hair and shouted that if Ong Ke Hien did one more thing to torture this child, she wouldn't answer for the consequences.

"Well," Ong Ke Hien said, "but—"

"Oh, get out, Glutton!" Ba Than yelled.

The three servant girls surrounded Thi Hai as she tottered off to her room on Ba Than's arm; one gained the impression that Ong Ke Hien would pay dearly for any mad attempt to break through this soft shield.

For a moment, Ong Ke Hien stood agape in the weeping ruin of his morning. Belgard, the neutral guest, had tried to blend invisibly into the woodwork while at the same time comforting Minh Chau, but Ong Ke Hien's unsettled old eyes discovered him.

Belgard gave a shrug that was meant to convey compassion as well as perplexity.

"But I scarcely eat enough to keep a lizard alive," said Ong Ke Hien.

"Wedding day," Belgard muttered. "Tensions."

"Yes, yes," sighed Ong Ke Hien. "Yes." He studied the streaks that still remained on the armoire and then he shambled out to the garden, where he fed the carp and talked to himself in a puzzled undertone.

"All right, let's see," Minh Chau said briskly the moment the old man was out of earshot. "What time is it? They'll be here at ten."

"*Glut*tony?" Belgard said.

"Now, my dear captain, if you're going to feel sorry for him simply because he's a man—"

"Why did Thi Hai feel sorry for you?"

"For us," Minh Chau corrected. "Well—and for him, too, really."

"For *him?*"

"It's been a long time since he made love to a young girl in a strange house." Minh Chau lifted Belgard's hand, touched her lips to it. "He was a very amorous boy, they say. Insatiable. But he's forgotten. He's acquired disinterest—which he calls wisdom. Thi Hai was afraid, I think, that he'd block himself into a corner with us, that he'd discover a truth he isn't equipped nowadays to handle."

"Thi Hai knows we were together then, last night."

"Oh, probably. Does it embarrass you?"

"No."

"Odd, isn't it?"

"Not odd. Sane."

Minh Chau's forefinger traced the line of his jaw from ear to chin. "My optimistic Don. . . ."

In the garden, the first guests had begun to arrive; they could hear Ong Ke Hien bidding them welcome, calling for iced drinks and betel leaves.

"Jack," Minh Chau said, and then pressed her forehead against his shoulder, laughing.

"What?"

"Nothing. It's just hard for me to say. Your name."

"To pronounce?"

"No, to *say*. I go along feeling so French, so modern, so emancipated—and then all at once, for some unexpected reason, I'm Vietnamese. . . ."

"What would you like to call me? What will Thi Hai call her husband?"

"Anh: 'Darling.' It's very intimate, very sweet. A newlywed word."

"And his name for her?"

"Em hai. When they have children, he'll become 'So-and-so's Father.' She'll be 'So-and-so-'s Mother.' " Minh Chau sighed. "How can I be a French rebel and a Vietnamese traditionalist at the same time? It's outrageous. But I am. My uncle told me before you came down how the Buddhists plan to protest if Diem continues his repressions. And, my God, it made my skin crawl, you know—and yet, I can *understand* it."

"Minh Chau," Belgard began slowly.

"No, I won't tell you what the plan is. I swore I wouldn't. It's terribly secret. It's designed to catch the world's eye—to evoke so much horror that Diem can't possibly survive. There'll certainly be a revolution. . . ." She shuddered. "I have my uncle's assurance that he won't take a personal part in it. I can tell you this. It's based on voluntary suicides—and even though my uncle begged to be the first, the leaders said no. They'll give some older monk the honor—or perhaps someone very young, very tragic."

The chatting and laughter in the garden died abruptly; the throb of gongs and the wail of pipes came to them from the direction of the road.

"Chérie, listen—"

"Sh."

The older men were entering arthritically, taking the best places near the altar, knocking each other about in their greed and haste. Minh Chau drew Belgard onto the veranda, clutching his arm tightly, as excited as a child. "Look, look—there's Van Tan—do you see him? Second in line, with the red and gold box."

Lordly and tall in his blue silk robe, Van Tan followed a young man who was laden with perilously balanced packages.

"The one in front," Minh Chau whispered, "is his best

friend, his assistant. He has the red robe and the circular hat for Thi Hai—gold earrings, rice alcohol—"

The two young men were flanked by two others holding long-handled mandarin parasols over Van Tan's head.

"What's in the red and gold box?"

"Mam trau cau—areca nuts and betel leaves. . . . The man behind Van Tan, the one who resembles a camel, is the Intermediary. He's arranged it all—cast the horoscopes, chosen the auspicious wedding day, mediated the bride price—very important fellow."

"And the ones carrying the black umbrellas?"

"Brothers, uncles, cousins of the groom."

The younger women came next, dressed in pastel-colored tunics, adorned with gold necklaces and thin gold bracelets. Those below the age of fifteen wore their hair loose and long; older girls displayed tight elaborate chignons at the back of the head. Next in line, grave and grim in raven-black garments, crunched the crones, guardians of the tribal morality, priestesses of duty and virtue. And last of all, like a New York cop on parade detail, hooded eyes alert for stragglers, walked Sergeant Grainger.

"Now," whispered Minh Chau, "the Intermediary will give Ong Ke Hien a little glass of rice wine and explain that they have come for the bride. Ong Ke Hien will be quite astounded at this—he may even protest that the girl is too young—but the Intermediary will win him over in the end with the mam trau cau."

When Belgard looked back at the courtyard, Grainger was still there, listening critically to the polite archaic argument over whether or not the girl would be surrendered. Grainger saw Belgard's eyes on him; he straightened and indicated over the heads of the crones that he needed to talk to Belgard at once.

"All right," Minh Chau whispered. "The bribery's worked; they'll be allowed inside."

"Chérie," Belgard said, "will you excuse me for a moment?"

Minh Chau glanced around and Belgard nodded toward Grainger, who bowed and smiled. Minh Chau returned her eyes to Belgard. "Who's that?"

"Don't worry," Belgard said. "There's nothing to worry about."

The guests were entering the house. Belgard threaded his way across the veranda and along the path to Grainger's side, and at every step his rage increased.

Grainger's face swam before him. "Captain—"

"What the hell do you want?" Belgard demanded in a low voice. "You're interrupting a sacred ceremony, do you know that?"

"I'm sorry—"

"Tell them I'll be back at the hospital on Friday."

"Sir—"

"Remind them I'm still on leave, Sergeant."

"Lieutenant Dodd called me."

You persistent bastard, Belgard thought, *get your finger out of my throat—this isn't lotus.* "I'll talk to him Friday."

"He said that Major Finney's on his way back. He's bringing a three-man commission to look the ground over. They'll confer with Colonel Tai and his staff—"

"There's nothing I can do."

"The commission especially wanted your recommendation. Dodd was under the impression that Finney assured them you'd be there—at the camp."

"Sergeant, it's already being taken care of—on the highest possible level! It's out of my hands."

"Yes, sir," Grainger said. "There is one factor working

for us, though, and that's time. They'll stay overnight in Ton That so Tai can throw a party and introduce everybody to his officers, and then they'll fly on to the camp in the morning. We could get out of Saigon by one or two o'clock and be at the camp before dark. You could wave him in from the paddy tomorrow, Captain. . . . Terrible sight for a man with a hangover."

The courtyard was empty; from inside the crowded house came the ritualistic drone of Ong Ke Hien's cracked old voice.

"No. It's academic anyway," Belgard said. "We'd have to wait for transportation north—"

"I checked with your friend in the hospital—Jackson— and he's arranged for a Heliocourier to pick us up at Tan Son Nhut. That's apparently a thing like a Piper Cub— Short Take-off and Landing plane. He said we could fly in with it fine."

"He did."

"Yes, sir."

Through the open front door, Belgard could see the lighted red candle gleaming in front of the altar. The wedding guests shifted and coughed in docile tension as Ong Ke Hien informed Thi Hai's ancestors of this new mating.

"Jeep's up on the highway," Grainger said.

"I'll be with you in a minute," Belgard said.

"Yes, sir."

The old dog was asleep on his reed mat, twitching and dancing away from multi-wheeled carts, when Belgard passed along the side of the house and entered the thatched kitchen annex. Pans bubbled untended on the fire; the goat had gotten in somehow and was drinking noisily out of a wooden pot full of shaggy yellow flowers.

The girl was waiting for him in Tinh Hoa's room. He

kissed her and explained to her what had happened, why he had to leave, and she nodded and said, absolutely, she understood. She said she would explain in turn to Ong Ke Hien. He promised he'd be back by Friday evening, and she nodded again and called him "Anh" and asked him to be careful.

He went back through the kitchen and along the side of the house, and walked beside Grainger up the path toward the highway. Once he said, "I don't know of anything lonelier in the world than a train whistle, do you?" and Grainger said, "Why? Did you just hear one?"

"No, no," Belgard said. "No. . . ."

CHAPTER 25

THEY REACHED Tan Son Nhut at a little past two in the afternoon, and while Grainger arranged to have the jeep returned to the headquarters pool, Belgard found a telephone on the observation deck and tried his best to coax the number of the Doc Lap pagoda out of a series of crisp young operators who gave him, in turn, the Pagoda Restaurant on Calmette Street, a Chinese law firm in Cholon, the Pagoda Restaurant again under its alternate number, and a family named Duc.

Grainger had rejoined him by this time. After the incident of the Duc family, Grainger pointed out that there was no special hurry, but that the pilot was ready now on the field, and Belgard told him through clamped teeth that by God no telephone company on earth had gotten the better of him yet, even the one in Westwood, California, and that this one wasn't about to beat him either. He dialed the fifth number, gripping the phone like a javelin, and to the "Allo?" he grated, "If this is the Pagoda Restaurant—"

"What? No, Doc Lap pagoda," said the voice impatiently, and the line went dead.

"Captain—" Grainger began.

"Just a minute, goddam it," Belgard snapped, and dialed again.

"Allo!"

"Is this the Doc Lap pagoda!"

"Doc Lap, yes!"

"Venerable Tinh Hoa, please."

"Venerable Tinh Hoa is not here."

"Do you know where I could reach him? It's very important."

"Who is this?"

"An American friend."

"Venerable Tinh Hoa was viciously beaten by Tyrant Diem's Brutality Squads in the holy city of Hué. It is not known whether he will live or die. He has returned to his ancestral home at Can Dop Cau. Are you an American newspaperman?"

"No. Listen—"

"Nevertheless, perhaps you know some newspapermen —perhaps some American senators. Are you acquainted with President Kennedy?"

"No—"

"In any event, let me send you some literature: the truth about Tyrant Diem, about Madame Nhu—"

"Listen, if Venerable Tinh Hoa should drop in there—"

"No, you misunderstand. He's in Can Dop Cau. He's hovering between life and death."

"All right—"

"Tell me, why do the American newspapers support Monster Diem? Why won't they print the Buddhist side?"

"I'm not a newspaperman—"

"Americans are historically fair, notoriously fair. They long to have both sides presented. But it's very difficult, you understand, to gain attention, newspaper space—"

"Well—"

"Though there certainly are ways. Butcher Diem forces us to strike directly at the world's heart. This intolerable suppression cannot help but result in tragedy."

Grainger coughed several times and allowed himself to be surprised stealing a look at his watch, and Belgard said into the phone, "Yes, well, if Venerable—"

"Venerable Tinh Hoa is more than likely dead. We have just heard the rumor that Thug Diem sent shock troops into Can Dop Cau last evening to burn and sack Martyr Tinh Hoa's home. Numerous young women were raped and slain, and several children were trampled to death by the enflamed troops."

"Enflamed and drunken troops," Belgard said wearily.

"What?"

"Nothing."

"We are attempting to verify this heartbreaking story now. Long Live Buddhism!"

"Long Live Vietnam," Belgard said.

There was a brief pause at the other end of the line, and then the voice said, "Yes, of course. Long Live Vietnam."

When Belgard had hung up, Grainger said, "Long Live *Vietnam?*"

"I was being a little snotty to a superpatriot," Belgard said.

"O.K., are we ready, Captain?" Grainger asked.

"Howard," Belgard said after a moment, "you've been in Saigon for the last couple of days."

"Yes, sir."

"Have you noticed any—increased tension over that Hué riot? Any demonstrations, or—"

"Captain, let me put it this way. After what I've seen

this week in this town, if I was Mr. Diem, I'd shave my head and get me a nice orange robe and a begging bowl and run for the goddam hills."

"What's the café scam?"

"A coup before the year's out, maybe before the end of the summer. The Buddhists don't *like* that man." Grainger eased away toward the stairs. "Sir, the pilot—"

"The pilot isn't going to go anywhere without us, Sergeant, so settle down." Belgard tapped his knuckles against the base of the phone, thinking. "He'd never in God's world try to arrest a leader like Tinh Hoa at this point. . . . Would he?"

"Well, Jesus, Captain, I wouldn't think so."

"He's pulled some strange tricks—"

Curiously Grainger said, "What's the matter, don't the monks know where he is?"

"Evidently not," Belgard replied.

"Well—"

The Public Address announcer asked first in English and then in French for Sergeant Grainger to report to the Information Counter, and while Grainger didn't respond to a word of the English version, he gave a leap at the fractured pronunciation of his name in French and cupped a hand behind his ear and shouted, "What? What?"

"They want you at the Information Counter," Belgard said. He'd already begun dialing. "Go ahead. I have to make a couple of calls. I'll be right here."

Grainger hesitated unhappily and then lurched off down the stairs.

The first place Belgard contacted was the motor pool, but no one there could tell him whether the young corporal who had driven him to Can Dop Cau had returned or not, and Belgard himself was more hindrance than help because he couldn't remember the corporal's name. He tried the hospital next. Grainger came back while Jackson's number was ringing, and Belgard raised his eyebrows inquiringly.

"That was the pilot," Grainger told him. "There's some kind of a weather problem. He's afraid they're going to ground the nonessential flights any minute."

"If Tinh Hoa walked into that palace last night, Howard, and nobody's laid eyes on him since, I damn well want the authorities to—"

The phone clicked in his ear and a female voice said, "Dr. Jackson?"

"Ah, yes," Belgard said. "This is Captain Belgard. Is Dr. Jackson available?"

"No, I'm sorry, he's with a patient."

"How long will he be, do you have any idea?"

"Why don't you leave your number, Captain, and I'll have him call you."

"Yes," Belgard said, "it's—" He caught sight of Grainger's apprehensive face and he paused. "I—don't suppose you'd break in on him for me."

"No."

At last Belgard said, "All right, thank you. I'll call back this evening."

Anxiety flickered in Grainger's pale blue eyes as Belgard replaced the receiver. "Call back from—?"

"Ton That."

"Ah."

A child in a scarlet coat ran heavily into Belgard's bandaged leg. He coughed in pain and tried to flex the agony away. The child sped off behind a whirring celluloid propeller on a thin long stick. Grainger had caught his upper arm in a startled grip. "Captain? What's the matter?"

"Rotten kid," Belgard gasped. "Son of a *bitch*—"

"What kid?"

Belgard twisted his head around. Grainger's uneasy form steadied as the waves of pain diminished, died. They were quite alone on the observation deck. "The boy—in the red jacket—"

"There's no boy up here."

Belgard rubbed his thigh gently.

"What was it, a Charley horse?" Grainger asked.

"Just a muscle spasm. It's gone now."

"I'll bet that hurt."

Belgard nodded and set out very slowly for the stairs. "The monk'll be O.K., Captain—don't worry about him. Diem can't afford to get the Buddhists any madder than they already are."

Belgard hesitated on the next to last step. At the ticket counter, a boy in a red school jacket hung sulkily from his mother's arm.

"Over here," Grainger said. "First gate."

After a moment, Belgard followed, head partially turned to keep the boy in view. Baffled, the boy fidgeted and ducked and stared back.

Just before they reached the gate, Belgard heard the running footsteps. There was no time to react. And even as the second child in the scarlet school coat rammed his bandaged leg, Belgard knew in his heart that it would never have happened if he hadn't been looking the other way, and that was the worst of the horror, that small new fact.

Because he understood now that *he* was the manipulator—that every move he made, either in wisdom or in panic, was creating the catastrophe, that even this special knowledge was foreordained, the fear, the hope, the rage, all foreordained, all unchangeable, all leading, like a cleverly numbered painting, to a broken neck and a burned woman and a military hanging on a gray Saigon-naise day before an invited puppet audience, watching out of wooden puppet eyes the final bounce and dance of the puppet that was him at the end of its ultimate rope.

CHAPTER 26

"You know what's wrong with this fouled-up hemorrhoid of a war?" the pilot demanded. "There's no ruttin' villains."

The icy air lay like a plastic sheet on Belgard's lungs; he could no longer feel anything at all in his injured leg. He had been given the seat next to the pilot out of deference to his rank, but Grainger, crouched behind and between them, could at least stretch full length when the cramp in his haunch became unbearable.

"You think about that," the pilot shouted over the engine noise. On his egg-bald head he wore a shapeless stocking cap, lovingly knitted for him, he had declared, by an eight-year-old Hong Kong whore named Deborah. "Who do we hiss? Ho? Come on, for Christ's sake, the old gentleman's a patriot and an underdog, and any red-blooded American who'd hiss an underdog has got to be a pretty dangerous pervert, Captain, now you *know* that. So who? Kennedy? Kennedy inherited the mess from Eisenhower. Eisenhower? Bite your *tongue!* The Cong's trying to unite his tortured land. The G.I.'s trying to honor a commitment. We're all being pulled hither and yon, Captain—hither, thither, and yon."

"Like puppets," said Grainger.

"Like fouled-up bloody puppets."

Smoke from hundreds of jungle fires drifted along the shattered canyons and mingled with the seasonal haze to half hide the toothy peaks alongside them. The Montagnards were preparing their hills for rice and poppies.

"There'll be a way out," Belgard said.

"Of this war?" shouted the pilot. "Never. We'll all be frozen with our hands around each other's throats. We'll all die cold and surprised, but we'll die."

"I don't agree."

"Captain, this isn't a nineteen forty-three movie. Don Ameche isn't going to win the girl. The girl's going to be decapitated in an air raid, and a defective gun's going to blow up in Don Ameche's face, and the last word everybody hears won't be 'love,' it'll be 'kill.'"

"If that's the script the audience buys, it isn't the producer who's sick, it's the audience."

"That may be—"

"And if that's the movie I'm seeing, Lieutenant, I'll walk out."

"That's the movie you're *in*, Captain."

"I can still walk out."

"Have you tried?"

"Hey, look," Grainger cried in tones of vibrant wonder, "what's that?"

"That," replied the pilot, "is a Moi village, Sergeant, and if arguments between officers disturb you, stop up your ears, but please have the goodness not to try to direct everybody's attention to another ring. O.K.?"

"How do you mean, sir?" Grainger asked.

"That'll do, Howard," Belgard said. The thatched huts cradled in the high valley below them had been newly built; the earth around was raw from recent slashings. Yet the village itself seemed as empty of life as a plague town.

The same image had occurred to Grainger. He caught Belgard's eye as Belgard twisted back to follow the wheeling land over his right shoulder. "Typhus?"

"No bodies—no disorder."

"There," said the pilot.

"Where? What?"

"Wasn't that somebody outside the longhouse?"

"That was a dog, wasn't it?" Grainger asked.

"No, I think it was a child," Belgard said.

"Do you want to take a look?" the pilot inquired.

"Let's make one pass."

The horizon tilted, drew them like tethered plumb lines to the left. They were in the valley, on their sides, crawling through the smoky air less than a hundred feet beyond the thick pine limbs. At the closed western end of the canyon, the pilot circled, straightened. They snored back toward the huts at eighty miles an hour.

"Anything?" the pilot asked.

"Not on this side."

"I don't even see the dog now," Grainger said.

"All right," Belgard said, "go ahead, Lieutenant, we can't fool around here."

"Funny business—" the pilot started to say, and the first bullet came from behind them and to the right, through the floor board and the loose fold of Belgard's trouser leg.

"Hey!" Grainger yelled. "What do you dumb bastards think you're doing!"

Witlessly Belgard gaped at the soldiers spilling from the huts. An officer in a long-billed cap ran from group to group, pointing a pistol at the airplane, directing the attack. He was very short, very excited; the pain on his face was religious. Twice he got in the way of his own riflemen, who were obliged to lower their weapons until he had lunged ecstatically away.

"For Christ's sake, why don't you climb?" Belgard shouted.

Slugs clattered against the engine. The windshield vanished and Belgard crouched forward, away from the pinch and slap of the air. Shrapnel shredded the floor at his feet. He heard Grainger grunt in surprise. "Howard?" he called. Blood sprayed across his lap and hands. "Howard!" He straightened and tried to look back, but Grainger shouted, "Get down, Captain! It ain't me! Get down!" and he was tossed to his left, against the pilot, who looked at him out of reproachful eyes over the tattered cavern that had been his lower face. The shrapnel had carried away the jaw and tongue and soft palate, but the man appeared to be unaware of this. He clearly believed himself to be talking to Belgard, perhaps to be reassuring him. The light airplane continued to buck sideways under the ground assault, wobbling now as the propeller was struck. The wobble alarmed the pilot. The expressive eyes sought out the instrument panel; the trained hands worked the throttle and prop controls. While Belgard watched, the oil pressure fell to zero.

On their left, a draw opened into a valley. They were beyond the village now, out of range, and now that it no longer mattered—now that nothing could ever matter again—their luck returned pointlessly, lavishly, gushing out like oil on the moon. As their RPMs dropped, so did the valley floor, stretching their glide beyond all reason, for mile after mile. Once they passed over a bald patch near an ugly stream, and Belgard pointed and shouted, "How about there?" but the pilot shook his mangled head and explained something in elaborate silent detail and gave Belgard a reassuring pat on the leg.

"Why the hell not?" Belgard called back to Grainger. "Do you know?"

"Logs? Tree stumps?"

"Were you hit, Howard?"

"No."

"We're going to make it. It's not our time—"

"Yeah, but like the man said, is it the pilot's time?"

The pilot heard him and waved, and the merriment in the eyes told them he was laughing.

"Oh, Jesus, Jesus," Grainger said and lowered his face to his hands.

The engine hiccuped, quit. The carpet of pines split ahead of them, and the pilot tapped Belgard's knee and nodded at the support pipes just in front of the instrument panel.

"Howard, can you find something back there to hang onto?" Belgard yelled. "We're going in."

"Oh, God," Grainger said.

The pilot cranked down the flaps, swung around in a lazy 270-degree turn. The deserted, scarred slope had been cleared perhaps a decade before, and an eight-foot-high cushion of bramble and bamboo had grown back in the interim. Seconds before their wheels dipped into it, Belgard remembered the shoulder strap he should have been wearing. He gripped the slick support pipes and thrust his back rigidly against the seat. The worm-covered door, set in a clump of bamboo, was partially open. It was raining in the courtyard and the guests were soaked and churlish. In a thoughtful moment, someone had draped a section of tarpaulin over the gallows so that Belgard would not get wet. He was alone on the platform. The chaplain, who had suffered from weak lungs since childhood, had waked that morning with a little cough and had had to excuse himself at the last minute. He had, however, sent a personal note to Belgard in which he had reminded him to submit to Jesus and not despair. He enclosed a pressed flower and several comforting Biblical verses written in a lovely hand.

They bellied into the crackling brown ocean. The pilot hit his switches. Slewing, bouncing, they ripped sidewise through the bramble, slammed to a stop. Belgard tore his hands off the pipes and rammed his shoulder again and again into the sprung door. The moist pungent odor of gasoline increased. "Howard! Give me a hand before this thing blows up."

The pilot, drained and dead, was in the way, leaning casually against Belgard's back. Grainger pushed the body aside, scissored his legs past Belgard's seat, and crashed his heel against the door in time with Belgard's blows. The door splintered, fell away. Belgard leaped out, reached up for Grainger. "Watch your eyes—"

"I know."

They staggered across the resilient trampolin-tough bramble patch to the edge of the jungle. A cloud of insects hung like a misty hump above Belgard's shoulders.

"Your jacket, Captain—they're after the blood."

Belgard stripped the jacket off and threw it into a bank of bamboo. The breeze across his bare forearms reminded him that this plane should have been equipped with survival vests. Heat from the engine shimmered over the broken wings in the bramble patch. There would be a sending and receiving radio unit in the vest—if there was a vest and if the vest could be found before the gasoline caught fire.

"Wait here," Belgard said. "I'll be right back."

"Where are you going? Captain?"

Belgard recrossed the springy snapping turf like a mystic on a bed of coals, at once benumbed and tender-footed. His calves, despite the protection of his trouser legs, were lacerated to the knees by the time he had reached the tilted door. He crawled in, telling himself that he was as safe as a child in a crib, that this was as foreordained as the rest, that he couldn't have it both ways, that if he was going to die on the gallows, then he was as immune from death by cremation as he was from death by tigers or death by Cong. But nothing helped. The stench of gasoline sickened him; the crackle of undergrowth outside and beneath the plane brought him time and again to a state of paralyzed anticipation. The dead pilot couldn't stop laughing at his antics. With every teeter of the plane, the pilot's shoulders would shake, the ruined head would hunch more deeply into the stiffening bloody scarf.

He finally found the survival vest in a tumorous-looking pouch that dangled like an Eskimo baby from the back of the pilot's seat. There was a pornographic snapshot in the pouch as well of a small nude Chinese child posing beside an artfully stuffed teddy bear and signed "Love, Debbie" in shaky block letters. Belgard put the photograph in the pilot's pocket, swung down into the bramble patch, and ran clumsily back to the jungle's edge.

"Did you find the flares?" Grainger asked.

"Flares—my God, I never thought of flares."

"How's your leg?"

"I'm all right. We're about—what—two miles from that settlement?"

"No more than two."

"They're bound to come after us. They knew we were hit." Belgard located a map in the vest, spread it on the ground. "Now—"

Grainger's finger indicated a large village in the western foothills. "Dan Ve."

"Right."

"Do you remember passing over this lake?"

"No."

"So—" Grainger squinted. "Let's say we're fifteen minutes out of Dan Ve—twenty miles, counting the playing around we did over the Cong settlement—the lake ought to be four to five miles due north—"

"Or less."

"Might be our best bet, Captain. He never got a mayday call off. Air Search Control won't have this location to nose in on."

Uneasily Belgard said, "I hate to leave the plane. If we miss the lake, we'll never in God's world be able to give 'em a visible landmark."

"It's a visible landmark for the Cong too. Question of who gets here first."

The tiny ASR-100 vest radio was about the size of a two-battery flashlight. Belgard hefted it, reread the specifications. Automatic homing signal—VHF and UHF—two-way voice radio—transmitting life approximately four hours. He raised the little antenna, pressed the switch. "Let's risk a couple of bucks on the Come Line, Sergeant."

"Yes, sir."

"Mayday," Belgard said. "Mayday—Mayday. Can you read me? This is Papa-Bravo-Xray—come in—"

"Is your squawk all the way up, Captain?"

Belgard increased the volume. "We'll give her ten minutes. Watch the clock."

"Go."

"Mayday—Mayday—Papa-Bravo-Xray calling Air Control—come in—"

Every thirty seconds, Grainger would nod his head and Belgard would fall silent for ten seconds, resuming the monotonous call again on Grainger's next nod. At the five-minute mark, they changed roles. But nothing bore results, even Grainger's thoughtful employment of obscene adjectives to lend color to an effort that struck both of them as basically artificial. It was as if they were too old for the game they were playing. Lines that had sounded rich and dramatic when they were children embarrassed them now. Belgard couldn't shake the notion that William Holden would gallop past at any moment, waving his rifle and shouting, "Come on, men! Let's get out of here!"

"O.K., ten minutes," he said, and Grainger pushed the antenna back and handed him the set, and with Belgard leading the way they waded north into the black and green jungle. Nearly an hour after they'd left the bramble patch, the airplane exploded. They stopped to watch the pillar of greasy smoke boil into the sky, and then they resumed their dogged march. In fifty-five minutes, they had covered a little less than half a mile.

CHAPTER 27

By dusk, it was clear that they had missed the lake.

Toward 1800 hours, however, they stumbled onto a matted path that reeked of tiger, and after weighing the pros and cons, Belgard decided that it represented greater advantages than dangers and suggested that they follow it. He felt that at worst their side arms could frighten any inquisitive cats away and at best the path would lead them to water. Grainger, on the other hand, said that it was just plain foolishness to tempt fate like that. He pointed out that this was a fresh run and that they were both too tired to be able to react in time to a stalking tiger. He was polite but very stubborn, and he insisted on a vote. Belgard voted for the path. Grainger voted against.

"Right," Belgard said. "Better luck next time," and started off down the path.

"Captain, wait a minute," Grainger said.

Belgard halted until Grainger had caught up.

"One vote for, one against—isn't that a Mexican stand-off?" Grainger asked. "I mean, this is a democracy, sir—"

"What did you call me?" Belgard inquired.

" 'Sir.' "

"This is a what?"

Grainger closed his mouth.

"Ready?" Belgard asked.

"May I change my vote, Captain?"

"By all means."

"I vote *for* the path."

"Good, it's unanimous," Belgard said, and swung off again down the trail.

The run led them north and somewhat east, along the edge of a ravine whose bottom was too distant and shadowed to see. At 1930 hours the final smudged trace of sunset was pinched off and the evening rain began, flooding the mountains in a theatrical downpour that made vision as well as coherent thought impossible. They found a vertical pleat in the cliffside that was too shallow to be a cave but that afforded them protection from the direct impact of the water. They huddled together in the violent darkness, bracing themselves against a sluggish odd heave under their feet, until Grainger said in Belgard's ear, "Captain, I think I'm standing on a snake."

"I think I am, too," Belgard said.

"He's a big bastard then—"

"Or we're in a den of them."

"I'm afraid that's it."

"Take hold of my belt."

Grainger hooked his fingers into the back of Belgard's pants, and Belgard eased across the muscular moving floor to the stream of mud that marked the tiger's run. The rain had lessened, though the blackness was as impenetrable as ever. "Are you out?" Belgard muttered.

Grainger had turned away, toward the ravine on their right, wracked by spasmodic vomiting. Sheet lightning pulsed through the sky. In the flare of it, Belgard saw—a yard or two farther on—a tree trunk bent over the cliff, ending in a web of branches that probably could support their combined weights. Ashamed, Grainger straightened, trying to wipe his chalk-pale face. "Can't help it," he whispered. He coughed and raised his mouth to the rain.

"It's all right."

"Snakes—"

"I know."

They inched sideways up the slick path, braced against the driving storm, coupled trunk to tail like two mad circus elephants lost in a jungle they no longer remembered. Belgard was aware of pain in his leg and belly, but it was a diffused aggravation rather than a wrench or an alarm or a trial. His outstretched hand struck the angled bole and he stopped.

"What?" Grainger said in his ear.

"There's a tree here. Give me your hand. . . . Feel it?"

"Yes—"

"I saw it in the lightning flash. We can climb it. It's not steep. It'll hold us both and we can get off the path."

"Good."

"The branches make a kind of platform about—oh—fifteen feet up."

"If our friend's in there, though, we're in trouble—"

"What friend?"

"El Tigre—"

"Lord, what a strength and a comfort you are, Sergeant."

"I think it's something we have to consider."

A gush of lightning surprised Belgard with his head turned away, toward the trail, but the hasty image he did manage to salvage when he swung back convinced him that the tree was empty. "O.K.," he said, "she's clear."

But the hand hooked under his belt had stiffened.

"Captain—what's the matter with you? Didn't you see him?"

"See what?"

"Captain, come *on!* There's a great goddam tiger up there, must be ten foot long—"

"Why, there is not!" Belgard said. "What's the matter with *you*, for Pete's sake?"

"Sir—"

"Howard, it's in your mind!"

"He's on his belly on that first big limb—"

"Howard—"

"I really don't know what you're trying to pull, Captain—"

"Listen to me—*listen* to me!" Belgard stared at Grainger's slack dough-colored face through the sheets of rain. "Now I'm *telling* you there's nothing up there! I'm *also* telling you that I'm not going to stay down here and drown in this bloody mud! I'll go up alone first. Do you want me to do that? Will that prove to you that it's safe?"

Grainger looked unhappily up past his ear toward the black platform.

Belgard tapped Grainger's shoulder, grinned broadly when he'd captured Grainger's attention. "Howard, don't you remember what I told you? They're going to hang me, man! So will you quit worrying about tigers?"

"Sir," Grainger said, "if you're putting me on, it's a very funny gag, but when this rain lets up, he's in one hell of a good position to jump us. Wouldn't it be better to just ease on down the trail for a—"

Enraged, Belgard gripped the trunk and hoisted himself off the path. Grainger lunged incredulously after him.

"Captain—this isn't fair. I can't get out of this place alone—"

The tree creaked under Belgard's weight. The rain

swept into his upthrust face, blinding him, clogging his ears and nose. He felt Grainger's despairing hand on his heel and he kicked free viciously.

About halfway between the trail and the first thick limb, the angle of the trunk increased. Belgard paused to catch his breath and to listen, but all he could hear in his wet black purgatory was the tearing sound of the rain through the leaves. Above him, a dead brown vine or a tiger's tail dangled from the crotch of the limb and the trunk, flicking in the gusty wind.

He gathered his muscles and inched upward. A lightning slash caught him with his cheek against the bole and his eyes closed. Thunder purred through the flooded sky.

He caught hold of the sides of the big limb. A paw, aimed well, could decapitate him. Teeth long enough could splinter his thin skull from crown to jawbone. Fighting, he clambered and scraped his way onto the rough rounded ledge.

The limb was empty. He clung to the main trunk in terrified disorientation, laughing and hiccuping into the wrinkled bark. He shouted Grainger's name two or three times, but these cries were exclamations of relief, like sneezes, rather than plotted attempts to communicate. The rain plastered his eyelids shut and drained in rivers down his back and legs. He crammed himself into the fork of the tree and tried to talk himself out of going back for Grainger. He reasoned that the son of a bitch wouldn't believe the truth in any event, that he'd probably argue in his martyred whine that Belgard hadn't gained the limb at all, that all of this hauling and tugging to get them both eaten by the tiger was nothing more than another of the lemminglike thrusts toward destruction that had motivated officers since the dawn of time.

It would be better to leave the tedious hillbilly stuck in his damned ooze.

He filled his lungs to their utmost limits and forced the air out between his pressed lips in a gigantic tired fartlike sound and made his dull body creep backward down the tree again to the ground.

"Howard!" he yelled. "Come on! I've been there and there's no tiger on the branch! Howard?" He thrust his arm through the black rain. "Howard!" He pivoted slowly around the tree, stretching as far away as he dared. "Howard!" He stopped. The rain drummed across his still face. He waited with one hand resting on the tree for the next lightning flash. There was no sign of Grainger anywhere, either on the path or down the slope. There were no other trees nearby and no caves—no hint, no clue to Grainger's presence or passage.

At last Belgard boosted himself onto the bent trunk again and returned to his perch. He sat in his safe high web and watched the heavy Asiatic rain fall in clots from the branches above him and wondered what it was that had come creeping up that spongy trail to bump into Grainger's undefended side. This is the wind that sent the cloud that held the rain that fell on the path that led to the tree that saved the man from the death that was meant for Sergeant Gr-a-a-a-ainger. . . .

CHAPTER 28

FOR THE WHOLE of the first day Belgard remained in his tree like a drab big bird, lightheaded, occasionally delirious. He had several satisfying talks with Minh Chau. She wore blue jeans and a short-sleeved white shirt, and she straddled the branch to his left and whistled through a blade of grass held in her cupped hands and discussed God and football with him. Once Grainger grabbed the tree from below and shook it, laughing, but went away when Belgard shouted that he was going to come down there and swarm all over him if he didn't quit it.

"Goddam fathead," he grumbled to Minh Chau.

"Well, he doesn't think, that's all," Minh Chau said.

"He never did, that's his trouble," Belgard said. "I could tell you some things about that man that would curl your hair—"

"Oh, look," Minh Chau said in a bright phony voice to distract him, "isn't that your lake?"

"What lake?"

"Where they were going to pick you up?"

"Where?"

"There—no, darling, look, look—this way—"

He blinked back at it in aggravated amazement. It lay in a depression just past the crest of the trail, not a hundred yards farther on. It had lost color and definition in the rain, but it was a lake all the same, and almost certainly it was the lake depicted on their map. "Well, I'll be damned," Belgard said.

"Isn't that funny?" Minh Chau laughed. "Here you were, right on top of it all the time."

Presently Belgard said, "Sweetheart, you know what it is, don't you?"

"What?"

"Well, it's a delusion. I'm delirious. I've felt lightheaded all day."

"Yes, but *I'm* not delirious," Minh Chau said reasonably, "so how come *I* see it?"

After a couple of false starts, Belgard gave up. "Can't argue with *that*," he said.

"Maybe Howard's waiting over there for us," Minh Chau suggested. "Shall we go see?"

"I don't know, I think we'd better stay right here where we're safe," Belgard said.

"Darling," Minh Chau said, "what are you talking about, *safe?* Safe from what? Inevitability? I really don't understand this crazy fight you put up. I think it's sweet, but I don't understand it. The fact is that you've peeked at the end of the book, you've cheated. Now, angel, it's all printed and you're *not* going to change cold type after all, are you? They're waiting for us. Ba Hoa for me and Ma Than Vong for you."

"Who in the name of Buddha is Ma Than Vong?"

"Ma Than Vong, darling. The Tightening-Knot Ghost. Haven't you heard him? Ma Than Vong goes around muttering 'Co, co,' into a person's ears to goad him into suicide."

"Muttering what?"

"Co. Neck."

"Oh, please—"

"Jack," Minh Chau said, "don't mock something just because you don't understand it. This *is* a suicide on your part, whether you want to face it or not."

"Why, it isn't either," Belgard snapped.

"Of course it is. You hang yourself in the end, don't you?"

"The *Army* hangs me!"

"All right, why?"

"Because I murder your uncle!"

"Exactly."

Belgard blinked at her smug expression of triumph. "Exactly what?"

"Well, *why* do you murder him?"

"*Well*—"

"Isn't it true," Minh Chau persisted, "that if you didn't murder him, none of this would happen?"

"Yes, but—"

"Then isn't it equally true that you must *want* it to happen? That it's voluntary, in the final analysis? A suicide?"

"But, my God," Belgard sputtered, "I don't want anything to happen to *you*."

"Why not?"

"Stop it," Belgard said. "Don't fish."

"No, I mean it. Why not?"

"Because I love you! You know that!"

"Now could it be, anh," said Minh Chau, "that you love yourself just a little more?"

"If I loved myself more," Belgard said, "I'd hardly kill myself. You aren't being consistent."

"But narcissism *is* selfishness, isn't it? And isn't suicide the ultimately selfish act? What does the suicide care for the tangle he leaves behind him—the baffled girls who cremate themselves, the misunderstandings—well, really, the wars?"

"No," Belgard said stubbornly. "No. No. You're not making sense. First you tell me that it's all inevitable, and then you say that it's all my fault."

"Both true—"

"Then you deride me for thinking I can change it."

"You deride yourself, chéri. You see that that part's simply a delusion."

"What do you mean, deride *myself?!* You can blame me for a good many things, love, but you can't deny that you started this fight."

"I do deny it."

"Minh Chau—"

"Anh," the girl whispered sadly, "whom are you talking to at this moment in this lovely tree?"

Belgard let his head fall back against the corrugated trunk.

"I'm sorry," Minh Chau continued in the same tragic whisper.

"You ought to at least allow me delirium."

"I said I was sorry."

"I suppose it's going to rain again all night."

There was no answer, and when Belgard opened his eyes, he saw that Minh Chau was gone. The sky was the color of putty, but clear; several stars already had appeared. He drew the small radio out of his shirt, stretched the antenna to its farthest height, and turned it on. "Mayday," he said. "This is Papa-Bravo-Xray—come in—"

Near the beginning of his third transmittal hour, two planes—a Porter and a Caribou—heard him simultaneously. The Porter, which was closer, made one fairly low pass directly over the trail, but the pilot had to confess that he couldn't spot Belgard in the dark. Belgard told him about the lake. The pilot said he could see that all right and promised to send a chopper down as soon as it was light. He was afraid that any more circling on his part would alert the Cong to Belgard's position, so he told Belgard to hang tight and take it easy and they'd see him at the lake at sunup.

Just before he signed off, Belgard said, "Now this is a fact, isn't it? I didn't make you up, did I?"

"Well, I don't think so," the pilot answered. "I guess we'll find out for sure tomorrow."

"I guess we will," Belgard said, and watched the blinking wing lights until they vanished like exhausted fireflies into the southeast.

CHAPTER 29

A TEPID WIND brushing through his treetop woke Belgard at a little past five in the morning. He felt hungry and depressed, but his lame muscles all responded when he asked them to, and his senses seemed dependable. He had one cigarette left, so he smoked that and watched the vague outlines in the ravine take on reality and substance in the milky growing predawn. When he could discern objects at least two hundred yards down the trail, he pinched the tiny cigarette stub out and eased slowly around on his branch.

The lake was there.

He sighed and leaned his cheek against the tree trunk and listened to the comfortable thud of the tree's heart and thought in a kind of delayed despair, *The tree's what?*

He drew his ear back and the thud grew more pronounced, better defined, approaching now from the southeast.

The lake was there, the chopper was coming, and he was up a tree sucking his thumb.

He jammed the radio deeper into his shirt and slid to

the ground. By then the big bird was visible, a huge H-34, painted brown. Splashing through the mud, stumbling from side to side like a drunk in a dream, Belgard fought his way to the lakeside just in time to see the helicopter sweep majestically across the opposite rim of the canyon. It continued north for half a mile and then settled into a motionless squat over a thicket of bamboo.

After he had screamed himself hoarse, it occurred to Belgard that he still had the ASR-100 and that a minute or two more of life might remain to it. He snapped it on and shouted, "Lake, you pitiful fatheads! Lake! Lake! Over here!"

The H-34 acknowledged his call with massive dignity but didn't move an inch.

"Don't any of you bastards know the difference between a lake and a grove of bamboo?! I'm *south* of you!"

The H-34 said yes, they knew the difference, and they'd be over there to try a landing on that level stretch to Belgard's left as soon as they felt that most of the Cong guerrillas were convinced that he was in the bamboo thicket.

"Guerrillas," Belgard repeated.

"Some of them are still headed toward you for some reason. You didn't happen to raise your voice when you called us?"

"Yes," Belgard said.

The helicopter soared abruptly upward and shot toward him. "We're on our way. We won't have time for more than one run. Good luck."

Belgard walked stiff-legged to his left, watching the chopper bore in over the ravine. Orders in Chinese came faintly from the trail below. The H-34 cracked into the ground, bounced. Belgard on the wrong side, zigzagged around the rear rotor. Hands were extended through the open doorway. Gunfire rattled over the lake. The chopper was already lifting when Belgard dove for the door. Two men grabbed him, threw him like a sack of grain to the other side. "My friend might still be somewhere around," Belgard gasped.

"What?"

"My friend! Can you look back down the trail—"

"Not now."

"Well, but—"

"We'll come back! When and where did you see him last?"

"A day, two days ago—"

"Could he have circled back to the plane? We found the Heliocourier with two bodies in it. They might have been GI—"

As the floor tilted and hurled him upward, Belgard could still hear the spastic popping of the Cong rifles along the path. One of his rescuers, a boy of eighteen with a bare bumpy shaven head, winked at him and said, "Tickets, please," and Belgard tried to smile back, but it was too hard, too complicated, and he fell asleep with his cheek on his forearm like a tired child after too much play.

CHAPTER 30

THERE WAS SOME question at first as to whether they should land in Ton That or go on to the larger base in Pleiku. The argument, which sprang up between the chopper pilot and the Ton That dispatcher soon after they were air-borne, hinged—so far as the pilot was concerned—on Belgard's need for rest and medical examination. He said the man had been through a terrible ordeal, that he looked very bad, that he tended to wander a little mentally, and that if G-2 was so frigging anxious to interrogate him why couldn't they send someone to meet him at the Pleiku field hospital? The dispatcher replied that he didn't cut the orders in this man's army, he just transmitted them, and was he to understand that the pilot refused to obey an acknowledged command here or what? Command from who, the pilot wanted to know, some frigging shavetail transfer from the C.I.A.? No, answered the dispatcher. Just give him a name then, said the pilot. Fine, said the dispatcher, how did Brigadier-General Ames grab everybody up there?

The pilot said that grabbed everybody pretty good and they'd be in in about ten minutes.

Belgard, who had heard fragments of the debate, kept trying to find out whether Grainger had shown up anywhere and what the present status of the Montagnard camp was, but the pilot felt that he had been put down and didn't care to resume contact with the dispatcher on any level but the most official and necessary. He advised Belgard to file a protest—perhaps through the Red Cross —and promised that he would back him up all the way to the Pentagon if it came to that. He said that if Belgard's health were permanently impaired by this frigging delay, he for one would call for Ames's court-martial.

"Well, that's kind of you, Lieutenant," Belgard told him, "but I really feel much better. I'm tired, but I'd just as soon be in Ton That anyway."

"What does Ames care about one life?" the pilot asked. "Not a frigging thing, he never did. Butcher Ames."

"Well—" Belgard started.

"Maybe they'll invite him to dance on your grave while they're playing taps."

"Right," Belgard said and leaned back and thought about Grainger and the chill faint line between illusion and reality until they spiraled down through the pine trees to their landing at Ton That airport.

The pilot's statements had borne some fruit, however, because there was an ambulance on the field to meet him when he disembarked. They took off, siren at full howl, the moment he was safely inside. While the corpsmen washed and dusted him with sulfa and replaced his caked belly and leg bandages with clean soft dressings, he attempted again to learn whether or not Tinh Hoa and Colonel Tai had been able to prevail against Finney.

"Well, I know they had a lot of trouble up there," one of the corpsmen told him.

"Has the camp been abandoned?"

"Oh, yeah, they pulled out—when was that, Earl?"

"Who, the Special Forces? Wasn't that day before yesterday?"

"Anyway," Belgard said slowly, "they're gone?"

"Oh, yeah, they're gone." The corpsman tapped his leg. "How does that feel?"

"That's fine," Belgard replied. "What about the Moi?"

"The—?"

"The natives, the Montagnards."

"Yes, sir?"

"I mean, are they all right? What's happened to them?"

"Now that I don't know," said the corpsman.

The ambulance barreled around a corner and came to a pompous bone-jarring stop in front of a commandeered pagoda watched over by two skinny young guards and a number of girls in tight short western skirts.

"Can we carry you in, Captain?" Earl asked.

"No, I can make it."

"All part of the service—"

"Thanks, I'm in good shape now." Belgard's head reeled when he heaved himself off the rear platform, but he waved and walked slowly past the girls to the pagoda steps.

"Nookey, duckey?" one of them inquired in English as he limped past.

"Go home and grow a little," Belgard said in Vietnamese, "and perhaps in five years I'll be in the mood."

Over her friends' surprised screams and laughter, the girl shouted in Vietnamese, "Five years for the mood, five seconds for the act, is that it?"

Belgard threw a wave of assent over his head and moved between the saluting guards into the building.

The cavernous main sanctuary had been partitioned into a hallway and offices. Belgard stopped a harried clerk and explained as well as he could what he was doing there, and the clerk said there seemed to be some confusion somewhere then because General Ames was in Pleiku, not Ton That. "This is Ton That, you know," said the clerk.

"Look," Belgard began, and then sighed and said, "Why do we always try to fight the machine, I wonder?"

"I couldn't say, sir," replied the clerk.

"O.K.," Belgard said. "O.K. Now. Where am I?"

"Ton That."

"No, I mean—what's this building?"

"Headquarters, Four Hundred and—"

"Who's your ranking Intelligence Officer?"

"That would be Major Niehaus, sir."

"Would you please direct me to Major Niehaus's office, Corporal?"

"Yes, sir." Tireless as a machine, patient as a mental therapist, the corporal set off on another of the endless mad tasks that filled his workday. Near the end of the central aisle, he paused in order for Belgard to catch up, pointed to the farthest door on the right, and said, "That one, Captain."

"Thank you," Belgard said. "Now that wasn't so difficult, was it?"

"No, sir."

"Do you see how much faster we move when we co-operate with the machine instead of flailing at it?"

"Yes, sir."

"When will General Ames be back, by the way—do you know?"

"Yes, sir."

Belgard waited for a polite instant, and then said, "Yes? Well? When?"

"As soon as Major Niehaus returns from Saigon, sir. Probably day after tomorrow."

Belgard scanned the serious helpful young face. "Major Niehaus is in Saigon."

"Yes, sir."

Belgard nodded, studying the scuffed muddy toes of his boots. Finally he looked up and smiled. "Well, I believe that's Game *and* Set for you, Corporal."

"Thank you, Captain."

"Not at all. Thank *you*."

The corporal saluted and vanished at a dogtrot. Belgard pressed his open hands over his face and told himself that he would stand here for just a moment longer and then he would inquire about beds, and space on choppers to Pleiku—Grainger could arrange that for him, perhaps, or —where was Grainger? His face struck the wall heavily, and a pincerlike attack on his fleshy upper left arm drew a grunt of pain from him. "Here, lower his head, lower his head," someone said in the distance. "Is he drunk?"

He fought the hand at the back of his skull. "Stop it—"

The lights increased in power; smells of sweat and smoke nauseated him.

"Just let me sit down—"

"Well, for God's sake," a familiar voice said. "Captain? Bring him in here."

"Who is he?"

"It's all right, I know him. His name's Belgard. Right here."

Someone gripped him under the arms and tugged him into Niehaus's office. His neck wobbled back; he squinted up into a pair of familiar nostrils. "Leonard?"

"Get him a doctor," Dodd said. He strained to see behind him. A chair kept scraping backwards as he attempted to swing Belgard into it.

"Leonard," Belgard said, "if you'd let up on this burlesque hold you've got on me, I could sit down by myself, honest to God."

"Here we go," Dodd panted and scissored Belgard sideways into the chair. "How's that?" He closed the office door on the curious faces peeping in and returned to look intently into Belgard's eyes. "You're white as a sheet," he said. "I wish you'd put your head between your knees—" He sat down opposite Belgard and automatically clasped one of Belgard's hands in his own, massaging it strongly and absently. "Jack, are you real?" he asked. "I tell you, this has been the worst son of a bitch of a week I have ever lived through in my entire life. The bastards said you were missing and presumed dead. No maybe, no pussyfooting around. Presumed dead."

"I presumed it on a couple of occasions myself," Belgard told him.

"Well, what happened?"

"We dipped in too low over a Cong village. They hit the motor—"

"How's your belly? I talked to the hospital after the operation and they said you were healing like a kid with a skinned knee, but I never know whether to believe those people or not."

"No, it's fine."

"Yeah? And the leg?"

"Fine, fine."

"Did they say anything about it?"

"Said I'd walk fine, no problem."

"Uh huh," Dodd muttered. "Well—"

"Oh!" Belgard said. "Listen, you should have heard that surgeon rave about *your* job."

"About my job?" Dodd repeated vaguely. The voice was casual, but the eyes glittered.

"He couldn't believe it when I told him the field medic had cleaned the leg out."

"Well, you know—I just did what I thought had to be done—"

"Well, he was certainly impressed, Leonard."

"Huh," Dodd said, chuckling. "I can't imagine why."

The room darkened; Belgard felt his elbow slipping off the arm of the chair. He bent forward. "Maybe I will—put my head down for a minute—"

"Sure."

The tape along his stomach drew and burned, but the flow of blood to his brain revived him. He said into his knees, "Len, what did you hear about Howard?"

"Just the same thing—that you were both down somewhere north of Dan Ve and presumed dead. Then Air Search found the plane and the two bodies and we knew that one of you had gotten out, but they said the corpses were too charred to tell much."

"One was the pilot—"

"The pilot and Howard," Dodd said, shaking his head. "Poor old Howard. Everybody's dying."

After a moment Belgard said, "Did they know for sure it was Howard?"

"Did you have somebody else along?"

"No, but I wondered if a Cong officer or somebody could have been in the plane when it finally blew up. They were following us. That's one explanation."

"For what?"

"What?"

"What's it an explanation *for?* I mean, do you think Howard might have gotten out?"

The cloth of his trousers against Belgard's nose still smelled of rain and bark. He thought of Minh Chau on her branch, whistling through her blade of grass. "No, I guess not," he whispered.

"What did you say?"

"Did they release the news about the crash?"

"No, but it got around—I don't know how. Somebody

said a girl phoned about it, about you. I believe it was a Vietnamese name."

Belgard sat up in the chair. "Was it Tran Minh Chau?"

"It could have been, yes."

"Can I make a call from here, Leonard?"

"Certainly." Dodd pulled the desk telephone over, lifted it.

"Where did the girl phone from?" Belgard asked.

"Saigon. Does the Doc Lap pagoda sound right?"

"Try that."

Into the mouthpiece, Dodd said, "Yes, this is Lieutenant Dodd. I'm speaking for Captain Belgard. I'd like to place a call to the Doc Lap, Saigon. I want to talk to a party named—" He looked questioningly at Belgard.

"Tran Minh Chau."

"Tran Minh Chau. Chau. I'm on seven seventy-three. Yes, I will, thank you very much." He depressed the telephone bar. "Anybody else?"

"A monk—Thich Tinh Hoa. But he's probably at the Doc Lap, too. Unless he's here in Ton That?" Dodd sat gazing at him so motionlessly for so long that Belgard finally said, "What's the matter, didn't you hear me?"

"Yes," Dodd said.

"Well?"

"Jack," Dodd resumed, "didn't anyone tell you what happened up at the camp yesterday?"

"About the withdrawal?"

"No, *after* that. We were out by Wednesday noon. I'm talking about Thursday."

Belgard regarded him wordlessly for a time and then shook his head.

"Jesus, I'm really lost," Dodd said. He got up and paced the length of the small office and came back to stand heavily in front of Belgard. "Why aren't you in the hospital then? What's the matter with these dingalings? They've been questioning all of us—Fox, Elkins, me. I thought that's why they brought *you* here."

"Maybe it was. Nobody said anything except that I was supposed to land in Ton That on Ames's orders."

"This is wild, wild," Dodd said.

"What do you mean, you were out by Wednesday noon?"

"That's right."

"*Wednesday* noon?"

"Yes."

"Well, what was all this crap Howard gave me about a commission coming up here on Wednesday to talk to Colonel Tai?"

"Yes, that was the *original* plan—but then Tuesday night Tai called Harkins's headquarters and said he had a strong request from Diem to abandon the camp. He said that Finney's projections had proved correct—that Ho had armed two more full divisions in the hills and that it would simply be a matter of murder to leave fifteen American soldiers there to face them. Somebody panicked —it wasn't Harkins himself; the thing never got that high—but the next we knew we were being evacuated by helicopter."

"That started Tuesday *night?*"

"That started Tuesday night, and by Wednesday noon we were all here in Ton That."

"While I was still in Can Dop Cau."

"Yes."

"What happened Thursday?"

"Now, Jack," Dodd began, "I want you to under-stand—"

"What happened Thursday, Leonard?" Belgard asked.

Well, Dodd continued in a low controlled tone, all of

this was secondhand, of course, and they were still piecing it together as additional reports trickled in, but the main facts at least had been pretty well substantiated. At sunrise on Thursday, two Cong guerrillas had come to the locked camp gate to ask for food. They said they knew the Americans had run away, and they warned the chief that they would have the village burned to the ground unless he let them in. They said they just wanted a few pigs and some rice and they'd be gone. They sounded legitimate, so after a little argument back and forth the chief decided that his warriors could handle two emaciated teen-agers and opened the gate.

There were twenty North Vietnamese regulars hidden in the fields. Half a dozen Moi were injured in the first volley, but by the sheerest accident the North Vietnamese officer in command was struck in the head by the answering fire and was killed. The result, oddly enough, was a partial disintegration on both sides. The Vietminh soldiers milled around for almost an hour, wondering what to do, but the Moi, who might even then have saved themselves, simply fled back to their huts and hid. A Vietminh sergeant rallied the soldiers at last, and they all marched in through the still-open gate.

("Leonard," Belgard got out, and Dodd stopped and said, "Yes, Jack?" but in the end Belgard just nodded and said, "No, go on, go on.")

The sergeant asked the first ten men he found to line up. He made a little speech about the tragic need to be severe where treason was concerned and read an excerpt from a tattered manual that listed the reprisal ratio at ten hostages for each dead Cong patriot, and then he personally shot each of the ten men in the temple, tears streaming down his cheeks the while. By this time, the soldiers had flushed most of the other villagers out of their huts and had brought the chief and his family forward for judgment. The sergeant called them his erring children and said that he would gladly give all he owned not to have to carry out the dreadful punishment the law demanded, but that he was helpless in the matter. He hoped, he said, that the onlookers had come at last to realize that the Long Noses were undisciplined and silly men who lacked the wit and the courage to help them in any important extremity. He asked the villagers to call out now, in a body, for Long Nose aid and compassion. When no one spoke, the sergeant repeated his request and explained that he was quite serious; he wanted to dispel any final doubt, he said, as to which side bore the mandate of Heaven.

The silence remained unbroken, and so the sergeant had to ask his own troops to play the parts of the villagers. Wailing, shrieking, the soldiers screamed for the Long Noses to shield the chief's son, to wrest the three-pronged disemboweling knife from the sergeant's hand. It was no use. While the seven-year-old boy's astonished eyes glazed in death, the soldiers' shouts rose in volume. Then at least, they begged, let the Long Noses send their touted magic to guard the chief's young wife. But they might as well have implored the tide to turn backward. The mother joined the child.

Now the sergeant gestured for silence. Holding the slick bloody blades in front of the chief's face, the sergeant asked whether or not the chief himself believed he'd been mistaken in placing his faith where he had.

In measured tones, but without the least hesitation, the chief answered, "Yes. I was wrong."

"Forgive your saddened Vietnamese brothers," intoned the grief-stricken sergeant, "as they have already forgiven you—" and plunged the knife deeply into the chief's vitals.

At this point, one of the huts had accidentally caught

fire. The sergeant, who until now had done a remarkable job under the circumstances, inexplicably panicked. He may have feared that the smoke would attract American attention or he may simply have reached the end of his emotional rope, but whatever the motivation for it, he had spun about and begun to run—by himself—across the camp, out the gate, and toward the hills. His men had followed in confounded disorder, and ten minutes later the village belonged to the Moi again. There was no question, of course, of anyone staying; the multiple deaths would have rendered the land taboo whether or not the political lesson had borne fruit. So the males had fired the remainder of the huts and camp buildings—which *did* catch the eye of a chopper pilot on his way to Ton That— and most of the tribe had returned to the mountains by the time the American scouting party arrived.

Dodd, searching for a cigarette, tossed his empty pack away and opened another. He tapped a cigarette out for Belgard, lit it, and slouched back to light his own, watching Belgard over his cupped hands.

Woodenly Belgard said, "Is that it?"

Dodd blew out the match and placed it in the exact center of the ash tray and then said, "No—not quite."

In their hasty withdrawal (Dodd went on) the Vietminh soldiers had committed one last military blunder. They had left their dead officer behind. And on the body, searchers had found two remarkable documents.

The first, from General Giap's Hanoi headquarters, exhorted the Patriotic Volunteers of the Mat Tran Dan Toc Giai Phong Mien Nam Viet Nam, the National Front for the Liberation of South Vietnam, to hold on and create happy thoughts of victory, as it was now a virtual certainty that Ogre Diem would be abandoned by the Americans before the year's end. The Patriotic Volunteers in the Pleiku zone could not be reinforced at this time, unfortunately, due to the barbaric American strafing of the neutral Ho Chi Minh trail, but the bearer was to expect news momentarily that would aid his recruitment program among the mountain savages.

The second document, a handwritten letter, was dated Tuesday evening. It stated that arrangements had now been made to evacuate the American Special Forces from the Moi camp outside Ton That and suggested an attack on Thursday morning at the latest. It said that Captain Belgard, the camp commander, was at that moment in Can Dop Cau, but that there was no guarantee that he could be kept there much beyond Wednesday. If he were to return to Ton That before the Thursday attack, every effort would be made to assassinate him, though of course positive assurances could not be given in that direction. This phase of the action, however, was to be arranged personally by Venerable Tinh Hoa, who had established good rapport with the subject and was sanguine over the outcome.

Belgard, aware that Dodd had stopped, raised his head.

"Tai's been arrested," Dodd said. "He denied having anything to do with the letter, but Diem had him returned to Saigon and the rumor is that he's already dead."

At length, Belgard said, "There's been a mistake. There are probably a thousand monks named Tinh Hoa."

"What?"

"He said he—knew the subject?"

"Jack, I'm sorry," Dodd said, "but I just can't hear you."

Belgard waited until the roar in his own ears had diminished. He pressed his thumb against the dull bruise under his breastbone and cleared his throat and formed each word as well and as loudly as he could. "Have they arrested Tinh Hoa?"

"I don't believe they have."

"Why not?"

"Well, what do you want—the official explanation or the pragmatic one?"

"Official."

"Officially, the United States and the Republic of South Vietnam intend to launch a thorough investigation into the suspicious circumstances surrounding the discovery of a document that might very easily have been planted on the dead officer's body in order to embarrass one of the most respected religious leaders in Southeast Asia."

"Bull shit," Belgard whispered.

"Yes," Dodd agreed, "but it's not bad for a spur-of-the-moment news release."

"And Diem agreed to this?"

"Jack, Diem's a fifteenth-century dictator, but he's also a gentleman. When someone hands a gentleman a cup of hemlock, he doesn't spit into it. He sets it on his knee and sips at it from the time to time and perishes as agreeably as possible."

"It was all so much easier when we were kids," Belgard whispered. "When they all wore black hats or white hats."

"Now all the hats are gray, aren't they?" Dodd said, nodding.

"What can Rusk be afraid of? The *Buddhists?*"

"Absolutely. Ever since the riots, it's been Suck-up-to-Buddha Week." Puzzled, Dodd added, "I don't know how I got so sidetracked, but I always thought Buddhism was supposed to be nonmilitant."

"So did Buddha."

"The insane part," Dodd continued, "is that the Communists *killed* half of Tinh Hoa's family in the old days."

"Stop thinking he's a Communist," Belgard said into his clasped hands. "The hats aren't Red either. Gray. Gray. Visualize gray. He isn't a Communist, he isn't a Buddhist. He's an anti-Diem politician."

"I'll tell you what this war could use," Dodd said. "Programs. Gitcha program here. You can't tell the traitors without a program."

The bruise in Belgard's chest had spread outward past the nipples toward his armpits. "Then you don't think he'll be arrested at all?"

"Never. Can you imagine the outrage in American circles if a Catholic president sanctioned the arrest of a brave, frail, lonely little Buddhist monk called Venerable Tinh Hoa?"

Belgard nodded.

"All right—" The phone rang and Dodd broke off to answer it. "Yes. . . . No, no, this is—well, who did you want? Oh! Yes, he's right here." He extended the phone toward Belgard. "It's the girl."

Belgard wiped his palm on his trouser leg and took the telephone and said in French, "Darling, are you there?"

The connection was crystal clear, brilliant, but the girl was crying too hard at first to be able to say anything at all.

"Em hai," Belgard said in Vietnamese, "don't weep, don't weep, please."

"You're safe—"

"Yes."

"Someone told me you were dead. . . . Is this really you, anh?"

"Really."

"I'm at the Doc Lap—"

"With your uncle?"

"No, he's in Hué—anh, what happened?"

"They withdrew the troops. The Cong came in and murdered the chief and his family."

Bewildered, Minh Chau said, "The—? Oh, my *God*. . . . But—no—I meant to *you*."

"The plane crashed, north of Dan Ve. A helicopter rescued me."

"Are you hurt?"

"No."

"Nevertheless, listen—you must stay in the hospital, you must obey the doctors. Would you believe that I knew something was wrong? I *knew*, before anyone told me anything—and then when they said you'd been killed, I swore at them, I really said the most foul terrible things, I called them—well, I can't repeat it—but chéri, when may I see you? Soon?"

"Yes, soon. I'll call the moment I return to Saigon."

"Today?"

"Hang on." Covering the mouthpiece, Belgard said in English to Dodd, "Am I stuck here, Leonard, until Ames or Niehaus gets back, or what?"

"What do you want to do?"

"Well, I think I ought to check in at a hospital—"

"I think you're right. To hell with Ames and Niehaus. I'll call the field, arrange flight space for you. You'll be in a nice clean bed in an hour." Dodd hurried out of the office.

"Yes, today," Belgard said into the phone in French. "They're getting a plane for me now."

"All right, I'll stay right here, at the Doc Lap. . . . Or do you want me to come to Tan Son Nhut? Or the hospital?"

"No, stay there. I'll call when I've landed."

"Good-by, darling—good-by, anh—"

"Good-by."

"I love you—"

"I love you. . . ."

CHAPTER 31

IT LOOKED LIKE the same C-47, but the pilot was an older, angrier man than Swanson. His name was Burke, and after the take-off he turned the controls over to his copilot and came back to ask Belgard if he happened to have a cigarette on him. He explained that he was trying to quit, but that he didn't think one now and again would hurt him, although he was damned if he was going to beg his snotty friend up front for a butt. He said he hated the little turd anyway, with his pale eyelashes and his offensive breath. He said he believed the man also wore a toupee.

Belgard opened the new pack he'd bought at the field canteen, and Burke, twitching like a marionette, lit up. Belgard urged him to take several more against the barren future, but Burke asked him what he thought he was, some kind of a weakling? He said it wasn't difficult to quit and anyone who claimed that it was was just a damned liar. If people would stop offering him cigarettes he'd have it licked in a week, he said.

Belgard shrugged and put the pack away and sat gazing out the window at the shadow of the plane fleeing the high slopes ahead and to their right. Presently he said, "The afternoon sun is on our left."

"That," Burke said, "is one hell of an impressive observation. It is on our left, yes."

"We're going north."

Burke looked at him for a while longer and then stood up. "Yes, we are," he said. "Your problem isn't mental, is it?"

"Saigon's south of us."

"Yes."

"Just where the devil are you taking me, Burke?" Belgard asked quietly.

"Captain," Burke said at last, "all they told me was that you wanted a lift to a hospital. Now if I'd have known your troubles were emotional—"

"I was supposed to go to Saigon."

"There wouldn't have been anything out of Ton That for Saigon until late tonight. Now why don't you just let the doctors at Hué look you over and then you can have a good night's sleep and maybe you can go back to Saigon tomorrow. O.K.?"

Belgard turned back to the window.

"Well," Burke said, "I guess I'd better get—"

"Burke," Belgard said, "sit down, for Christ's sake— can't you tell when you're being put on?" He looked around and grinned and pulled out the cigarette pack again. "Sit down, sit down, sit down."

Burke pursed his lips and then chose a cigarette and bent over for Belgard's light. "I'll tell you," he said, "you were just a *little* too broad, you know?"

"Come on, I really had you going there."

"No, you didn't."

"Like hell I didn't."

"Well—I thought, what's so bloody bad about Hué? I mean, a hospital's a hospital."

"Right," Belgard said.

"And I knew they wouldn't have made an appointment without telling you."

"Oh, yeah," Belgard said. "I knew about the appointment." He leaned against the curved cold frame of the ship and gazed north and east into the haze that China hid behind. "I've known about the appointment," he said, "for a long, long time. . . ."

CHAPTER 32

THE HOLY CITY of Hué, sleepy and subversive, lay like a spilled armful of blocks along the non-navigable Song Huong, the River of Perfumes. Age and civil strife had combined to gnaw leprously at its streets as well as its temples, and the ambulance that had been dispatched to pick up Belgard apparently had tumbled into a hole and broken an axle. Belgard was assured that another would be along shortly, however, and in the meantime why didn't he check in at the Red Cross wagon and have a nice cup of coffee?

Belgard said thanks, he believed he'd just do that, and strolled out to the parking lot, where he hitched a ride to the Tourist Office on Ly Thuong Kiet Street and rented a bicycle. There was no need to ask directions; he simply put his head down and pumped, gliding along with the traffic as peacefully as a man in a punt on the Thames. He knew in a dreamy way where he was going. He even knew there was danger at the end of the trip, but this was an academic problem, comparable, rather, to the gradual swell of the earth miles and miles below a free-falling sky diver.

The building he came to was small and made of stucco. Hibiscus and bougainvillaea had spread untended up the low walls and along the roof. A skinny cow grazed in the courtyard.

Belgard rested his bicycle against the side of the building and walked up the three long steps to the paved veranda. He was studying the shattered French doors when a tip-seeking caretaker in a black turban and a black cotton tunic over white trousers hobbled up to him and told him toothlessly and without preamble that he supposed he was interested in the riot; well, the riot had begun, in fact, exactly at 8 P.M. He was certain of that because he had happened to turn to a friend seconds before the monk had started his exhortations, and had asked the time, and the friend had stated it was precisely eight o'clock.

"And you were where?" Belgard asked.

"I was inside, your honor, but I could hear everything. These doors were open at that time—although later, when the crowd began to curse and to press forward, the Station Director grew frightened and locked us all in. . . ."

"I see."

"The monk wanted the Director to broadcast certain tapes he had, but of course that was out of the question."

"Why?"

"Well, they were treasonable, you understand. Anti-government political slogans—"

"You're sure of that?"

"Oh, absolutely! The monk told the crowd what was on the tapes. And they grew more and more passionate, angrier and angrier—so the Director telephoned for help —armored cars—but by then it was too late; the crowd was out of hand, breaking windows, screaming for us to play the tapes—"

"Then the monk was responsible for the riot?"

"Oh, yes."

"And did he—or any other Buddhist—ever try to calm the crowd?"

"Certainly not."

"Do you know who this monk was, old man?"

"It was the Venerable Tinh Hoa, your honor."

(Down and down he fell, feathery and free, while the benign earth inflated like a pretty balloon.)

"Yes, go on," Belgard said.

"Well—so then the Assistant Province Chief arrived. But he couldn't get his armored cars into the courtyard. Stones were coming through the windows. I hid my head —and at that moment I heard two explosions, very, very loud—then gunfire—then ten or fifteen smaller explosions—"

"Grenades."

"Yes—and everyone was screaming—and when we ran out to see what had happened, we found the bodies, seven or eight adults and a child. It made me want to vomit, your honor. The tops of the heads had been blown off, you see—"

"By MK III concussion grenades? Not possible."

"Well, that I don't know, but the heads were gone. All the other wounds were above the chest—but do you know, we couldn't find any metal. . . . We couldn't understand it. Grenades are made of metal."

"But the Cong plastiques aren't," Belgard said. "Are they."

"Plastiques," repeated the old man. "No. . . ."

(Down and down and down, close enough now to see the configuration of the mountains and the fields, the homely wrinkles on the loved old face.)

"Where is the main Buddhist pagoda from here, old man?" Belgard asked.

"Well, of course there are two, your honor, Thu Duc

—231—

and Cho Len."

"Thu Duc."

"I'll show you."

Belgard hand-rolled his bicycle out of the courtyard behind the hobbling caretaker and listened gravely to the complex unintelligible directions.

"Then right at the third—I beg your pardon, the *fourth* corner—then left—right again—no, no, I'm wrong—"

"I'll find it. Thank you."

"Thank *you*, your honor!"

He left the old man bowing in delight over the size of his tip and launched himself back into the irregular stream of traffic, peddling evenly and absently over the cracked cobblestones.

Ahead of him barbaric sounds drifted on the gray air, odors of jasmine and joss. A tall gate stood ajar. He dismounted and leaned his bicycle against the wall. Something screamed *Anh, Anh, Anh* and then *God* in French. A burned figure began to topple toward rubber-soft asphalt.

He pushed through the gate.

CHAPTER 33

HE WALKED INTO a courtyard crowded
with old women in black pajamas and bald saffron-robed
monks. A boy scout said in tortured English, "Americans
—Number Ten," and spat in his face. Two slender Vietnamese girls covered their mouths and giggled as he
passed.

He shouldered the hostile jostling beggars aside; if he'd
had a club he'd have used it. On the crumbling pagoda
steps, under a profusion of Buddhist flags, stood a tiny
nun. She smiled tenderly at him through betel-blackened
teeth and pressed a soiled paper tract into his hands.
"Youth of Vietnam," it read, "be ready to sacrifice yourself for Buddha and drive the Americans into the sea."

"Bonjour, mon vieux," someone said.

He looked up toward the jagged peaks of the pagoda
scratched against the sky. On the second-floor balcony,
Thich Tinh Hoa fingered his amber beads, a tall frail man
enveloped in a gray robe. The bones of his face and
shaven head were as tense and delicate as crystal. "What
do you want, Captain?" he asked.

"You were expecting me, Tinh Hoa," Belgard said.
"Don't ask ridiculous questions."

"Very well, then," Tinh Hoa said. "The girl called. But she said you were in the hospital."

"You see that I'm not."

"You're a very sick man, Captain. You ought not to be out of bed."

"I'm coming up."

"Why?"

"You know why. The letter. Why did you betray me, Tinh Hoa?"

"What letter? Betray you how?"

Belgard started past the tiny nun, and at the same time a young monk smelling of onions grabbed him from behind and pinned his arms to his sides. He jackknifed forward. The monk's feet stumbled against the stone steps; the large peasant backside slapped the ground heavily.

Thich Tinh Hoa shouted an order down in Vietnamese, but it was too late. Grease shone on a blunt dagger the young monk had dug out of his orange sleeve.

(*Anh, Anh, Anh,* screamed the voice.)

"Use it," Belgard whispered in French. "Try."

The monk's black eyes remained fixed on his. Wind rustled through the torn paper banners pasted to the stucco walls. On the fringes of the crowd, children demanded explanations in piping voices.

The monk lifted himself like a snake, straight upward, mute, barely swaying.

Thich Tinh Hoa repeated his strident order.

"They'll think you're afraid," Belgard whispered. "Try."

The point of the knife touched Belgard's chest.

"Do you understand what I'm going to do?" Belgard continued. "I'm going to snap his neck like the stem of a flower. You could stop it, coward—"

The dagger shot forward. (*God,* screamed the voice.)

Belgard sank back and gripped the wrist, corkscrewing the monk across the fulcrum of his leg. (Horns drowned out the howl—the strident Edsel, piercing Peugeots and Citroens.) Spectators scattered. The monk landed on his stomach and rolled over, eyes to the sky, both arms broken. A pedicab driver drew the saffron skirt chastely over the bleeding knees.

Thich Tinh Hoa hadn't moved by the time Belgard reached the balcony. People poured through the iron-grill gate into the courtyard below, ants converging in greedy anxiety on a broken orange honeypot.

"I think you're insane," Tinh Hoa said. "Let me call a doctor." It had begun to rain a little; dark spots appeared here and there on the gray robe. "Come inside—"

"I want to know why you betrayed me."

"Yes, let's talk about it in the reception room. I have a soft sofa for you to lie on." He placed his arm around Belgard's shoulders. "Now what's all this about a letter?"

"She didn't tell you?"

"All she said was something about the Montagnards near Ton That—"

It was raining harder now, but he continued to resist Thich Tinh Hoa's efforts to lead him inside. Over the tap of the rain on the wooden overhang, he thought he could hear a siren. He walked to the edge of the balcony. An American Army patrol wagon nosed through the press of people at the main gate. A wave of nausea overtook him. He caught hold of the iron railing—

"Come along, Captain," Tinh Hoa wheedled. "Come inside, mon cher, hm?" Skeletal fingers plucked at the cuff of his jacket. The skin over the long bones was pale and translucent.

Turning, tears coursing down his cheeks, Belgard screamed over the miles and the weeks to the tormented blackened figure, *"Em hai!"* and broke through the low railing backward into the rain.

The figures below scampered for safety; Tinh Hoa stared after him, aghast.

He fell like a drunk, like a sky diver, released, relaxed, crazy with fulfillment, smiling at Tinh Hoa through the gentle rain all the way down. . . .

Schultz